Fic
Hob   D

DATE DUE | BORROWER'S NAME | RM. NO.

Siskiyou County
Office of Education Library
609 South Gold Street
Yreka, CA   96097

50584

DOWNRIVER

·WILL HOBBS·

BANTAM BOOKS
NEW YORK · TORONTO · LONDON · SYDNEY · AUCKLAND

To David Brower who led the fight in the 1960s that saved the Grand Canyon from dams and reservoirs in Marble Canyon and Lower Granite Gorge

"I want to ask you to do one thing in connection with it in your own interest and in the interests of the country. . . . Leave it as it is. You cannot improve on it. The ages have been at work on it, and man can only mar it. What you can do is keep it for your children, your children's children, and for all who come after you. . . ."
—*Theodore Roosevelt, on his visit to the Grand Canyon, 1903*

RL 5, age 10 and up

DOWNRIVER

A Bantam Book / published by arrangement with Atheneum

PUBLISHING HISTORY
Atheneum/Macmillan edition published 1991
Bantam edition / July 1992

The Starfire logo is a registered trademark of Bantam Books, a division of Bantam Doubleday Dell Publishing Group, Inc.
Registered in U.S. Patent and Trademark Office and elsewhere.

All rights reserved.
Copyright © 1991 by Will Hobbs.
Cover art copyright © 1992 by Robert McGinnis.
No part of this book may be reproduced or transmitted in any form or by any means, electronic or mechanical, including photocopying, recording, or by any information storage and retrieval system, without permission in writing from the publisher.
For information address: Atheneum, Macmillan Publishing Company, 866 Third Avenue, New York, NY 10022.

ISBN 0-553-29717-1

Published simultaneously in the United States and Canada

Bantam Books are published by Bantam Books, a division of Bantam Doubleday Dell Publishing Group, Inc. Its trademark, consisting of the words "Bantam Books" and the portrayal of a rooster, is Registered in U.S. Patent and Trademark Office and in other countries. Marca Registrada. Bantam Books, 666 Fifth Avenue, New York, New York 10103.

PRINTED IN THE UNITED STATES OF AMERICA

RAD   0 9 8 7 6 5 4 3 2 1

I STUMBLED ON A ROCK THAT WAS BARELY sticking up, my legs were that tired. Flailing for balance, with the pack working against me, I slipped in the mud and almost went down. I still couldn't believe this was really happening. I couldn't believe my dad had done this to me.

For five days Al had been leading us into the most rugged corners of the San Juan Mountains in southwestern Colorado, coaxing and pushing us over the passes and into the peaks, through good weather and bad weather, mostly through bone-freezing rain and sleet. "October in the mountains," Al said with a grin. "You live a whole lot closer to the edge."

The going was always either straight up or straight down—we rarely followed trails. There were eight of us, four guys and four girls including me, all serving nine weeks in this outdoor education school from hell. Al called his program Discovery Unlimited, but we called it Hoods

1

in the Woods, the name we inherited from the previous waves of misfits who'd come through the place.

Al kept us marching all day under heavy packs, grinding us down in preparation for . . . for what? He would never say when you asked him. He'd only reply with a wink or a knowing grin. Hike, freeze, starve, break out the ropes and carabiners and risk your life every day—for what?

"Just a mile till camp, guys," Al said. "Think about a sunny day."

I couldn't. I could see nothing but the frightening dark tunnel that was my future. I saw no images there, no hopes, only blackness. All my happy images lay in the past, all the happy scenes with my dad when it was just the two of us. I tried to dwell on the good times as I walked, but those pictures, those voices, only intensified my feeling of loss and left me staring once again into that black tunnel.

"How's it going?" Suddenly Troy was walking at my side.

"Okay, I guess."

"You don't look so happy."

"I'm ready to be in camp. When Al says a mile, you know it's two or three."

"It's part of his charm."

We jumped a little creek and started up a steep slope. Soon neither of us had enough breath to speak, but thinking about Troy took my mind off me. He seemed much older than the rest of us, just from the way he carried himself. It was like he was sizing up this whole situation from the outside. I'd been wondering if he was going to be friendly, and now it seemed he was.

Camp at last. I found a dry spot under a tree and eased

my back against its trunk. Troy sought me out and sat cross-legged, up close. "Does the climbing scare you, Jessie?" He was looking at me with the calmest and clearest blue eyes I'd ever seen.

"Yes," I allowed, looking away.

"I thought so." He said it knowingly, in a way that promised help. When I looked back to his eyes, they kind of locked on to mine and wouldn't let go. Apparently he never needed to blink, and he wasn't going to look away. His eyes seemed to be challenging me to . . . to what?

"I'm doing okay so far. . . ."

His eyes let me go. For now, I thought. I was fascinated by him. Someone was yelling that he was supposed to be one of the cooks. Troy reluctantly unwound his long legs and said, "Catch ya later."

We drew in close to the campfire that night, putting off as always the moment when we'd have to get into our freezing bags and face the shivering hours of the night. We knew Al would make his speech about the next day and of course he did, as he poked the fire. "We've got the climbing skills down now, guys—it's time for a true test. After that we'll head back to base camp for hot showers, real food, and our beds."

I pictured the little log cabin that I shared with Star, and how good it would be to stoke the potbellied stove until the stovepipe turned red. So what was this big test going to be?

"Tomorrow," Al announced, "you're going to climb Storm King Peak, elevation thirteen thousand, seven hundred, fifty-two feet. And it's no puppy. You'll know you've accomplished something. We'll draw straws this evening

3

for climbing partners. Troy, you're going to be the navigator—you haven't led yet."

"Nothin' against Troy," Rita said in her nasal, right-at-you New York accent, "but if this Storm King is such a big deal, why not let Freddy lead? We know *he's* good at it."

I glanced over at Freddy. The campfire light flickering on his deep brown skin, black eyes, and shaggy black hair revealed, as usual, nothing in the way of response. True, I thought, he's capable, but he's practically mute. I'd much rather follow Troy. I had reason to believe that Troy cared whether I lived or died.

Al was shaking his head emphatically as he spread the topographic map out on the ground. "Troy will do just fine. He's your leader for the climb. Star, you're shivering—come into the light and warm yourself up. Folks, everybody needs to develop these skills, every one of you. Sometimes there isn't going to be anybody else around."

"But we travel in a pack," Adam pointed out with his trademark mischievous grin. Our redhead loved nothing better than sidetracking a conversation. "So whoever's going to lead can study the map and the rest of us followers can go to bed."

"Seconded," said Pug, the Big Fella, stretching one giant leg out toward the fire and nudging a piece of wood into its center.

Al scratched behind an ear, amid the wiry gray hair that stuck out beneath his wool cap. He was rocking slightly on his haunches; he preferred to squat rather than pull up a log or a rock. He reminded me in his body language of an aborigine or a tribesman from the Amazon, right out of one of the slide shows my dad used in

4

his anthropology classes. "Sometimes," Al said slowly, "sometimes self-reliance is the key to survival, but other times cooperation is. Let's everybody study this map, and then tomorrow, on the mountain, we'll pool our knowledge. Whenever somebody's wondering if you're doing the right thing, bring it up with Troy."

"What if the right thing, the way we figure it, would be to go into Silverton for burgers?" suggested Adam.

Everyone had a smile or a laugh, including Al. With Adam, there was never anything at stake. He was so easy.

I could sense Heather getting ready to object, and I braced myself for her voice, which I found jarring and oddly mismatched with her broad shoulders. When she thought something was unfair, which was most of the time, her voice rose even higher than its usual pitch and her speech came out squeaking and gasping, because she couldn't talk and breathe at the same time when she was upset. "What I don't get is, we can all cooperate on the climb, right, except for you, Al. You won't help us at all, right?"

"That's what this is all about, Heather—you guys have the skills now. You make the decisions, you make the choices, you live by the consequences. You'll be on your own. I'll just tag along for the scenery."

Troy, I noticed, was attending to all this. Watching, listening, but withholding comment. Everybody was looking to him, including Al. Troy was a heavy, and everybody knew it. We were all wondering when he'd take Al on, but he was holding back.

When Heather saw that Troy wasn't going to respond, she said in that voice like an abused violin string, "You say we get to make the decisions, but really we're just puppets, and you're manipulating us. I don't like your rules, Al. I can't accept that you get to make them all up. Who gave you that right?"

That's telling him, I thought. That's exactly how I feel. This guy reminds me of my dad.

"Right on, sister!" thundered Pug, who was only half-listening, his attention focused as usual on his biceps. Despite the cold, he was wearing a T-shirt cut off at the shoulders, and was admiring the firelight's reflection on his muscles. Without thinking about it, he proceeded to punch Troy playfully in the arm. Maybe it was Pug's way of showing gratitude to his buddy for bestowing his nickname, the Big Fella.

"Why don't you blow your whistle, Heather?" suggested Adam with his wide ironic grin. "Blow your whistle, loud and clear."

When you blew your whistle it meant you wanted out, it meant you were going home. I'd been wondering all week when somebody was going to do it. I'd sure thought about it, about getting out of this place. But I figured out why I hadn't done it: aside from not wanting to be first, I would have had to face what I'd be going back to. Was there "home" back there for any of us?

I could only answer for myself. As for the others, their lives were mysteries. We were as far apart as galaxies in the night sky. Star and I shared a cabin back at base camp, yet I had little sense of what kept her going. She seemed so frail, I'd have guessed she'd be the first to blow her whistle. If the last week had been torture for me, what must it have been for her?

Some stayed up into the night, talking by the firelight—Heather, Rita, Adam, and Pug—and the rest of us either listened without comment or tuned out. Star was in a trancelike state, and I was far away in my mind, reliving an awful day less than two weeks past that was a wound I was sure would never stop bleeding. I was back in my bedroom upstairs in my house, the same bedroom that was mine even before my mother died back when I was five, and there was only an hour to go before Dad said we had to leave for the airport. I was looking at all my kid stuff, clutching my timeworn teddy that I'd named Pistachio for no particular reason when I was little. I was trying to lose myself in the old photographs on the walls. Only one photo of my mom, lots of me, but mostly pictures of me and my dad together, at Disneyland with Goofy, on horseback in the mountains, at the beach, all over.

I stood by my bed, holding on for dear life to the brass rails and looking out the dormer onto the street. I thought of how many times I'd planned to escape by way of the window out onto the limbs of the elm tree, but instead slipped out the kitchen door because it was so much easier and because Dad wasn't catching on anyway. Now, within an hour, I'd be leaving my home forever, and Dad would pack everything up in boxes, including all my things in this room, and he would move on with his life to the canyon home he'd designed with his girlfriend, and this life I'd known would all be swept away.

As for me, he was sending me away. No matter how much he denied it, that's what he was doing, and I threw it back in his face a hundred times. He just wanted to believe the therapist, who told him this was what I needed—to discover myself, learn my limits, all that psych talk. It just made him feel better about getting rid of me. More time for him and Madeline.

"It's only nine weeks, Jessie," he said. "And it's not like you don't love the mountains. You like hiking, remember?"

"Hiking?" I could hardly believe he was still trying to sell me this propaganda. "This is a program for juvenile delinquents, Dad. It's not summer camp."

"There'll be different kinds of kids there, Jessie. This program is one of the best in the country. Your school counselor, your therapist, we all think it'll help you find yourself, rediscover the wonderful girl you used to be, help you grow up. I know growing up is hard, I remember. . . ."

"This is all Madeline's idea, isn't it, Dad? Admit it. You know she's friends with my counselor at the high school."

We'd had this argument so many times before, I knew which lines came next.

"That's not true. Madeline cares about you too. We're worried about your safety, Jessie; we don't want you to get hurt, or to hurt someone else."

You'd think no one had ever rolled a car before. It was an accident, one that could have happened to anyone. And not just to a kid, either. The police had blown it all out of proportion. We weren't drunk. And we were way out in the country, where there shouldn't have been any other cars.

"You're worried about what people will think of you at the university because your daughter is hanging around with 'bad company.' That's it and you know it. The big professor. Just because my friends look different—you think they're not good enough for me."

"Jessie, there's a lot you don't know about those guys. I

see them on campus, and I know more about them than you do. They're too old for you, honey—you're just a sophomore in high school."

"I *was* a sophomore in high school—I told you I'm not going back. I hate that place."

"Jessie, what can I do? You tell me. You don't come home, you've been in two car accidents, and you're not even old enough to have your driver's license yet. The school calls constantly, you aren't in classes. And this is just the first month of school—last year you did so well. I don't understand, Jessie, and you're scaring me. I'm afraid of what you'll do next."

In a perverse way, I liked that part, about how I was scaring him. I knew I was, and it went straight to my head to know what I could do to him. The bitter things I'd said over the past months were nothing compared to what I said in our last week. When I heard myself saying, "I hate you," I swallowed hard, but I never took it back. I wanted him to suffer, and I knew him well enough to know that's exactly what he was doing.

Then the time arrived. I heard my dad call from downstairs, "It's time to go, Jessie," and then I burst into tears, desperate to hold on to everything I was losing. I would never stand in this room again, never sleep in this bed again, never look out these windows again. I had a picture of my dad and me in my hands; I threw it down onto the hardwood floor and the glass broke with a finality that frightened me and seemed to push me over the edge. Every one of those pictures of the two of us, I threw them down onto the floor, and every time it made things worse. I was breaking my own heart over and over again.

Suitcases in hand, I walked down the stairs into the house that was holding its breath. My eyes were all cried out. My cat was at the bottom of the stairs at the front door, eyes darting from me to the door and back, frightened and wanting out. Dad was sitting there on the couch, his heart all broken, and I said into the silence as coldly as I could, "Let's go."

The awful silence captured every moment as the familiar streets and neighborhoods disappeared behind us. For my part, I was fighting in the most hurtful way I could think of, by feeding the silence and making it grow and grow. I knew how badly my dad was hurting. There was nothing he could say. He needed to hear a word of understanding, a word of forgiveness from me, but there was no way I was going to provide it.

As we got out of the car at the airport parking lot, my dad tried again. "Al—the guy that runs the program—believes that our culture lacks a ritual by which young people can decisively achieve adulthood, and that's why a lot of us never seem to grow up. It makes a lot of—"

"Save it for your graduate students," I said.

Inside we were striding briskly down the concourse. I looked straight ahead, down into that black tunnel that was my future. Again we couldn't speak, until we reached the door that opened out onto the runway where the little "flying culvert" was waiting, when my dad hugged me and cried, and said, "Jessie, I love you." I forced myself to look at him, and said, "Yeah, well, give my regards to Madeline," and I broke away from his grasp and walked out to the commuter plane without looking back.

· 2 ·

THE NIGHT BEFORE STORM KING, I GOT NO
rest. I was whirling and tumbling inside the car with the
world spinning out of control all around. I woke up and
took a drink from the water bottle between Star and me.
It was pitch dark, still the middle of the night. When I got
back to sleep, I was climbing a mountain with Troy and
some people who weren't even in our group. I kept saying
that we should turn back, we were late for something, but
Troy wouldn't. Then I slipped, and was hanging from his
grasp for the longest time, but then he let go and I was
falling, falling, falling.

Thrashing around in the tent, I woke Star. "Are you
okay?" she was asking.

"I'm okay," I said, barely coming to. "Just fell off a
mountain, that's all."

"That's not good, Jessie."

"Well I guess not, seeing as how we're going to be

11

climbing a peak with ropes and all that stuff in a few hours."

"Imaging can make things happen," she whispered. "You have to work on your images."

"It's not like I can control my dreams, Star. I've had falling dreams since I was little."

What I didn't tell her was, they started right after my mother died. I'd told her enough.

Unable to get back to sleep, I lay shivering, and wondering if my dad had any idea that I still get those dreams. I told myself that the nightmare had nothing at all to do with actually falling, or with mountain climbing. Skiing doesn't scare me, flying doesn't either. Mountain climbing, I told myself, I can do that if I have to. If *Star,* for crying out loud, if Star can do it, then I can too.

At breakfast I drew Freddy for my climbing partner. I was relieved. As withdrawn as he was, he wasn't an exciting companion, but he was a capable climber, probably the best among us.

The eight of us, with Al trailing, set out from the trees at dawn, trying to make as much time as we could before the weather turned bad, which it tended to do every day around noon. Troy, our navigator for the day, led the way, along with Heather, his climbing partner.

When we cleared the trees, we couldn't see the peak. A high ridge, serrated and imposing, blocked our view. Troy started up the ridge, making good time. He didn't stop to look at his map and he didn't ask anyone for a second opinion. I wondered if we should be "conferencing," the way Al wanted us to, but like Troy, I was anxious to get on with it before the weather turned bad. Already the clouds were boiling up out of the blue skies.

I walked three steps behind Freddy. I felt awkward with him. Freddy was not exactly an artist when it came to conversation. Anyway he seemed content to ignore me. I had the feeling he was something of a wildman, and I was a little afraid of him, like maybe he had a violent streak and had committed some awful crime. He was the only guy, I noticed, that the Big Fella wouldn't wrestle with and sit on whenever he wanted to play or show dominance or whatever it was. Freddy had some kind of signal that said "Don't touch," and even Pug, the sensitive soul that he was, could pick up on it.

Freddy slowed a bit, and I thought for a moment that he wasn't sure if we were going the right way, but he said nothing. I stopped and caught my breath. Freddy sniffed the wind, like an animal. He did that often. His jet-black eyes would focus, never on the people, but on the clouds and the peaks, on little gray birds flitting around, on rocks and dirt and trickling water. Someone said Freddy was from New Mexico. When Freddy did speak, it was in a musical Spanish accent. Like Pug, he never flirted with the girls, but unlike Pug, he didn't joke around with the guys either. Freddy was a loner.

As I caught my breath, I watched Troy's bright shock of blond hair bobbing as he chattered with Heather. I wondered what they were talking about.

I was enjoying the walking, happy to have left my enormous backpack in the trees and feeling weightless by comparison, with only my daypack on my back, even if the slope was getting steep and the air thinning by the moment. We were somewhere around thirteen thousand feet, heading for close to fourteen. Al bounded alongside us, appearing out of nowhere with a huge grin plastered across his face and a cheerful "Great day, isn't it!" He wasn't even breathing hard. He's in his mid-forties, like my dad, and strong and lean as a whip. Even his gray hair is like that, I thought, springing out like steel wool from under his cap and jumping out of his nostrils and ears. There were moments when you almost wondered if you liked him, but those were the rare moments he wasn't killing you, and they passed quickly.

"Say, look at this," Al said, and swooped to pick up a bit of bone, something I would never have had the energy to notice while climbing at thirteen thousand feet. "Power object!" he proclaimed.

Freddy, looking vaguely interested, slowed up as Al held it out for us to look at. "Bird bone—hollow. What do you think, Jessie? You're a Colorado girl, from Boulder and all."

"I'm too winded to even speak," I managed. "How am I going to think?"

"Freddy?"

My climbing partner shrugged.

"Maybe a bit of Mr. Raven's wing, chewed by Mr. Coyote," Al theorized. He kept looking at Freddy as if Freddy should really know. Then he took the leather pouch that hung from around his neck, opened it, and dropped the bone fragment in among the rest of his "power objects," whatever they might be. I could never tell if Al was as weird as he sounded, but I guessed that he was. He was always grinning. I had my own images of Vietnam vets, maybe from seeing too many movies, but I knew I didn't trust him. I didn't buy his premise that taking kids out in the mountains and making them suffer will fix what ails them. And to live the way he did, year in and year out, he had to be a madman. I sure wasn't going to respect him for it. So I was always off balance with him.

I looked around for Star and Adam, but they were well behind. Adam would have milked some comedy out of the "power object."

It wasn't time for fun, it was time for technical climbing. We'd run out of walkable ground. Al dropped back to take up the rear on our "true test" and leave us to our own devices. As Freddy took his coil of rope off his shoulder, Troy waved us around him and Heather. The clouds were turning dark and the wind was suddenly blowing hard. I could see the uncertainty in Heather's body language even though she avoided my eyes. Words rarely failed her, but on this occasion she didn't say anything. Her partner motioned toward the face of the looming peak and said, "You lead, Freddy. Find us a route."

I watched Troy as he said it. It was a tough admission for him. He was such a natural leader and such an able person physically. It was a defeat, having led all the way from camp, to have to follow now. I glanced to Freddy, to see how he would take it. He shrugged.

We broke out our nylon climbing harnesses and rigged them snug. Mine dug into my crotch a little. I hated it. I thought about how my father had never done any technical climbing in his life and yet had blithely shipped me off to Hoods in the Woods, knowing that climbing was a lot of what they did. Carefully I secured the rope to my harness. "Check my knot for me, would you, Freddy?"

He looked me all over. "Okay," he grunted.

Frightened, I adjusted my helmet with the strap under

15

my chin, and looked to Troy for reassurance. My fear had boiled up out of nowhere like the clouds, and I could taste it. Troy's eyes skittered away for once. He bent over and busied himself getting his rain gear and his helmet out of his daypack.

"Oh well," I thought, "here goes nothing." I can't believe that was my attitude, given my fear and my nightmares, but I'd always liked to push myself. Driving too fast, that goes without saying. Wanting to hang out with older guys. I'd wear all white, I'd wear all black, I'd wear my hair long, cut it off short, put a purple streak in it just for fun. I wasn't afraid of what people would think. My dad liked to say it was a natural stage that he had gone through too. "Young people tend to see everything in extremes, not only in our society and not just in modern times—they always did." Anthropologists talk like that. He's studied cultures all over the world, but mostly in books. He hasn't done any field work in his beloved Amazon since my mother died.

"You think in extremes, Jessie," he liked to tell me. "Everything's either wonderful or it's 'blown.'"

Freddy led the way, climbing easily if not gracefully, pausing here and there to hammer pitons into the rock. His stocky body seemed to hug the earth naturally. I'm Freddy's height, but I'm hollow-boned like Al's raven and naturally defiant of gravity. I have a long-distance runner's stride, I've always been able to leap and jump, and I've always liked skiing because it set me free, left me attached only marginally to the ground. Now as we started across the face of this peak, the depths were pulling powerfully at me from below, and I felt my strengths turning to weaknesses.

"Don't look down," Freddy cautioned from above me.

16

His warning came too late. That's exactly what I'd just done, glanced at the drop. It had to be a thousand feet. I'd seen the sharp boulders jutting at crazy angles at the bottom of Storm King Peak's north face, and they seemed to be rushing up to meet me.

"Jessie, don't look down."

Too late. My stomach was in free-fall already, and I was so dizzy I thought I might black out. Suddenly lightning broke from the blue-black sky and thunder exploded almost instantaneously, with all the force of a sonic boom.

I was aware of gasps and swearing from the rest of them. I knew I hadn't been hit by the lightning, but all the same the sheer terror of the moment chased the strength from every fiber in me, and I was paralyzed.

I glanced up. There was Freddy, with his shaggy black hair blowing in the wind, his face all lit up with a feral sort of joy born of the wild moment. Whoever he was, my life was now tied to his, and our eyes were locked together. He said, "You can do it, Jessie. Move your right foot to that little spot over there, and your right hand to that finger hold."

"I can't," I whimpered.

From behind me and below I heard Rita, the self-proclaimed Thief of Brooklyn, holler the loudest stage whisper I'd heard in my life. "Jessie's got that 'sewing machine leg' Al talked about."

It was true. I was so afraid, the nerves in my right leg were buzzing and the leg was twitching up and down.

"Take a few deep breaths," encouraged Al. I glanced down and back toward the ridge, and saw an impression of his face, wide-eyed under his helmet.

"Look at that leg shake!" I heard Pug yell from below. He obviously loved the spectacle of the jumping leg but had no idea it was connected to my feelings.

"Pug," Freddy called down, "keep your mouth shut."

Pug yelled something back at Freddy. I could feel the spasms in my leg—I didn't need to look. What was worse, numbness was spreading through the rest of my body.

"Everyone cool it except Freddy," ruled Al. "He's her climbing partner." I looked back and below, the way I had come, looking for Troy. He was the only one I could trust. I was hugely relieved to see him appear behind Pug and Star. "Troy . . . ," I said desperately, "I'm in trouble. Help me!"

"Let me catch my breath," Troy answered.

I looked up at Freddy, saw him grinning. His teeth flashed whiter than white against his dark skin and jet-black hair. Lightning snapped again, and the wind began to blow hard. "Whistle through your teeth and spit," Freddy offered. "That's what my father always used to say."

Great. That really reassured me. I'm about to black out, about to fall off a mountain, and my only hope is this sawed-off criminal wildman who wants to make some kind of a joke.

"I can't whistle," I muttered. I didn't know if I was more terrified or angry. None of this would be happening, I thought, I wouldn't even be here . . . if it weren't for Madeline. For nine years it had been just me and my father, and then *she* marched into his life and ruined everything.

I was standing in what should have been a temporary spot, a little ledge wide enough for one foot, but both of mine had ended up there. I couldn't go forward and I couldn't go back. My center of gravity was out beyond the ledge and above that bottomless drop. Only my fingers held me, and the longer I clung to the rocks, the weaker they'd become. Now they'd gone numb, buzzing and weak and about to let go. I felt as helpless as when my mother died. Daddy, I thought, your Sugar Plum is about to fall.

I looked for Al once more and found his startled face. His expression confirmed my conviction that I couldn't hold on any longer. "Troy!" I pleaded. There was no response. Why wasn't he doing anything?

"Gotta make your move, Jessie," Freddy urged. The encouragement did a poor job of masking his alarm.

"I can't," I cried. I had no strength. "It's a discovery program," I heard my father saying. "Jessie, you need to find yourself."

As the clouds dropped and boiled around us, I felt the eeriest sensation: My hair stood out from my head and all of my body tingled with electricity. A moment later lightning struck again and thunder shook the mountain. The rain broke, and the storm center hurled violent wind gusts and sheets of hail against the peak.

"Go for it, Jessie!" ordered Al's voice, and finally I did, with no confidence at all. I made a lunge to the right, with my hands and a leg, and tried to grab hold of something, anything. For a moment my fingers scraped and clawed, my feet dug for a hold, and then I was falling.

Suddenly I was caught up and spun end-over-end somehow, with my head down and my legs above me. My helmet banged against the wall and I was looking straight down its dizzying slick face.

"I got you!" Freddy yelled.

The climbing harness around my hips and between my legs dug in painfully. My life was in Freddy's hands; he was belaying me with the rope passed behind the small of his back, mustering whatever strength he could in his arms and shoulders, back, and legs. If he let go, maybe the piton anchoring the rope would hold, maybe it wouldn't.

"Hang on!" yelled Al. "Hang on, Freddy! I'm coming around!"

I heard the others react, the ones waiting behind and below. They were frightened and thrilled at the same time, as if they were witnessing a spectacular auto accident. "Hold her! Hang on, Jessie!" Star called.

"No way," Pug said. "He's not going to make it in time."

"Don't say it," I heard Star plead. "You'll make it happen."

Something was keeping Al. Star told me afterwards that he was having all kinds of trouble climbing above and past me, by another route, to Freddy's position.

My hands reached out and fended my body off the cliff. "Freddy!" I screamed, as I freed my face from the wall. "Freddy!"

"I got you!" he hollered. "I got you!" His voice came out kind of strangled. I knew he was barely managing to hang on to me when I heard that.

All the blood had rushed to my head. I was dangling there forever. It was taking too impossibly long. The way everyone was shouting, I knew Freddy must be losing his grip. Any moment now, he'd have to drop me. I was so bewildered. *Was I going to die?*

Star told me afterwards, Freddy was a sight to see. He's not that big, but he has wide shoulders and narrow hips, and all the muscles in his arms and neck were standing out like whipcord. She said she's never seen that kind of determination in her whole life. It did take forever, she said, but somehow Freddy held on, until finally Al scrambled down next to him. The two of them hauled me up enough so that I could right myself and work my way back across the ledge to Troy's grasp and safety.

An hour later the clouds opened and the sun shone on Storm King Peak. We were down below, having bailed out. No one—not even Al—brought up going for the peak after what had happened. So we'd failed what was supposed to have been the big event of the first stage of Discovery Unlimited.

The rest were having a raging fight as they were eating lunch by the sign at the base of the mountain, the one that says,

> **WARNING:**
> STORM KING PEAK IS INFAMOUS
> FOR ITS EXTREME WEATHER,
> EXPOSURE, AND ROTTEN ROCK.
> THREE HAVE DIED HERE.
> THINK BEFORE YOU ADD
> YOUR NAME TO THE LIST.

People were yelling about how it all happened and what we should have done. Rita was born with a set of lungs, and she was exercising them in spades. A couple of octaves higher, Heather played her screeching violin for all it was worth, as if she could shred Al with her voice alone, while Pug thundered curses and bristled back and forth like a grizzly bear uncertain whether it was bluffing or charging. But most of all there was Troy. I'd never heard his voice raised before, and was he angry. "What do you *mean* having us climb that lousy mountain? Man, look at the sign! Three people died on Storm King! You coulda got Jessie killed, idiot!"

"You picked the route, Troy. And it wasn't the one we planned last night."

I was confused. So were the rest—they fell silent.

"Whaddaya mean?" Pug demanded.

"The map, Troy. I guess you chose not to use it. That was a harder route than the one we discussed."

Such a volley of curses I've never heard in my life.

"How come you didn't say something?" Pug asked.

"Troy was the navigator today. You all know the rules."

"I can't believe it!" Rita shouted, beside herself. I looked over there and saw her right in Troy's face. "I can't believe him and I can't believe you! You took us up the wrong way! We coulda all been killed. Why didn't you look at your map, Troy?"

Troy walked off. I couldn't blame Troy. Nobody else had helped him out. It was Al I was angry with, for risking my life just because of his stupid rules, angry at my dad for letting him do it, and hating Madeline. I went over what I was going to tell my dad as soon as I got to a telephone. "Get me out of here," I rehearsed through clenched teeth. "Get me out of here!"

With a start I looked up and saw that Freddy had sought me out. I was jumpy. What did he want?

He didn't say anything at first. He sat down on a rock and looked out across the meadow, turned red and gold with the hard frosts of early October. He was watching a pika, a little animal like a ball of fur, scurry from rock to rock with a bunch of grass in its mouth. "We call 'em rock rabbits," he said finally.

I didn't say anything. I wished he would leave me alone. Obviously he thought he was entitled to hit on me because he'd saved my life.

"You know what he's doing with that grass?" Freddy asked in his musical accent.

"No, I don't know what he's doing with that grass," I said flatly.

He looked at me like maybe he would leave, but he explained, "They don't hibernate—they run around all winter under the snow. They have to have something to eat, so they cut grass and dry it all summer, and take it underground. They're hayfarmers."

"I never heard that before," I said sarcastically. "Now if I say 'thank you,' will you leave me alone?"

He was really embarrassed. He stood up quickly. "I just wanted to—oh, forget it."

He left. And I felt like a complete heel.

· 3 ·

TROY AND I WALKED TOGETHER ON THE long hike from Storm King back to base camp. We lagged behind the others so we could talk. I was feeling defeated, pretty sorry for myself. "I don't know what to do," I told Troy. "I want to call up my father and scream at him, but if he lets me go home, you can bet it'll be on his terms."

"Forget about your dad for awhile," he suggested. "The mountain-climbing part is over, anyway, and we're heading for the desert. I'm really looking forward to the river-running, myself. I love water."

Being with him was so soothing. I asked, "What kind of water stuff do you like?" I wanted to learn all about him.

"Are you ready for this?" he said with the most engaging smile. He was handsome, sure enough, with his blue eyes, sun-bleached blond hair, and slim build. Usually he seemed so much older and more serious, but at the moment he was positively boyish, and I found it irresistible.

"What is it? It can't be that weird. I'll bet you don't sell aquariums door-to-door."

"Surfing."

"Why didn't I think of it?" I laughed. "You're blond, you're tan. . . ."

"And I practically grew up on the beach, in San Diego. I love moving water, Jessie. I've always thought I'd like whitewater rafting. . . . There was a guy I knew at the beach, an older guy, best surfer I ever met—he always talked about rivers being the ultimate. He used to talk about the rapids in the Grand Canyon all the time."

"So does Al," I said, "but we aren't going to the Grand Canyon. We're just going to the San Juan River, and it's supposed to be pretty flat."

"Gotta start somewhere, and it'll be warm out there, Jessie. It's in the desert."

"That's what Al keeps saying."

"Just promise me one thing."

"Yes?"

He reached out and touched my cheek, "Don't blow that whistle. I don't want you to leave."

I laughed. "I would hate to be the first one."

"Don't be afraid, Jessie. There's nothing like new experiences in life. What are you, sixteen?"

"Almost."

He shrugged. "In a lot of countries you're grown up when you're thirteen. Your father's trying to psych you out so he can stay in control. He wants to put you through something, tame you down, so you'll play by his rules."

"Well, it's all down the tubes now."

Troy let it drop. Troy was the most sensitive guy I'd ever

25

met. He watched and he listened much more than he talked. His eyes did the talking. "Trust me" was what they said.

I scrambled to bring the conversation back to life. "You seem awfully independent. Were you raised that way?"

"I guess you could say that. My parents are pretty much on their own trip—they live in Europe, do a lot of traveling. I have a couple of sisters, but they're a lot older than I am. I hardly know them, really. I guess I was kind of an afterthought—or an accident, more likely. I lived with my grandparents when I was a kid, and then got sent to different boarding schools in the East."

"Sounds like it must have been pretty hard on you. . . ."

He shrugged. "There was good and bad, I guess, but I came out my own person."

He had such an easy way of talking, like his way of moving. Natural grace. A laid-back, unconceited self-confidence. "I admire your independence," I told him.

"Like the song says, 'the past is just a good-bye.' "

"I feel so humiliated about what happened back on the mountain. I was absolutely terrified. That's never happened to me before in my life."

"Forget it," he said easily. "Just another experience. You move on."

"Because of me, nobody got to the top."

"I thought I was the one who got to feel guilty about that, remember? Picked the wrong route?"

"No, it was my fault. I just panicked. Everybody has been good about not saying so, but we all know it would've felt great to be standing on the very top of that mountain."

Troy was pained. "That's exactly what Al would like

you to think. I can't believe the guy's judgment. He should never have put you or the rest of us in that situation. We don't have the experience."

"But that's what outdoor schools do."

"You know what I think? It's all a power trip. They create this situation where they can turn you into putty. They scare you to death and then they save you. I don't know about you, but I'm sick of people playing God with my life."

"You can say that again."

We walked up on the others, who were standing around uncomfortably, trying to take the weight off their shoulders without removing their packs. Al would rarely allow a pack break. From the looks on their faces, it was obvious even from a distance that they'd been waiting for us to catch up. "What's up?" Rita said. "You two having your own private experience?"

Pug snickered. I didn't say anything. Rita would love to have Troy's attention; so would the others, especially Pug. People looked up to him and wanted to get closer to him. He granted his favors sparingly, which meant they were all the more in demand.

Somebody, I noticed, was missing. "Where's Freddy?" I asked.

Al called Freddy's name a few times, but no answer came. Freddy was like that, a loner who could vanish on cat's feet. During basic training, before the Storm King expedition, Freddy would disappear from camp whenever we had free time. We had a day off before the big hike, and he was long gone. I was relaxing on the cabin porch in the hammock that afternoon, when I noticed a solitary figure climbing above timberline toward a gap in the peaks towering above the camp. I'm sure it was Freddy.

"What if he splits?" Pug asked Al. "What are you going to do about it?"

"I'm not worried," Al said. "Freddy'll be back." He wasn't about to launch into a "what if" discussion with Pug.

Pug laughed. "And if he doesn't show up, it's between him and his probation officer, right?"

I wondered if Freddy took off because of me.

My mind shot back to my predicament on the cliff face, and I saw Freddy once again on the other end of the rope. "I got you! I got you!"

I felt bad, I felt confused. I had every reason to like Freddy. He'd always had a good word for me in his bashful way, and I'd been so cruel. I thought about Troy's reaction on the mountain, when I was pleading for him to help me. Why hadn't he even tried? He'd fallen silent, seeming as paralyzed as I was. I put it out of my mind. There probably wasn't anything he could do.

Underway again, Troy and I kept up for a while, then lagged behind once more. The weather was building again, and the sun was gone. Visiting with Troy, I didn't even care that it was cooling off and threatening to rain. "Adam's a kick," I was saying. "He doesn't take himself seriously."

"Adam doesn't take *anything* seriously."

"You're right. He can turn anything into fun."

"Here's one you'd appreciate. . . . Back in his home town in Kansas he would actually dress up like a Ninja, robe and sword and all, and sneak around at night, climbing trees and prowling rooftops, and he'd come in through girls' windows and leave roses on their pillows."

"He could've been shot!"

"I guess," Troy said.

"Did he ever get caught?"

"Sure, that's how he wound up here, but you know Adam . . . he didn't take that seriously, either. He's a bit of a space case, but in a different way than Star. She's in *deep* space, wouldn't you say?"

I had to think for a minute about how to describe Star.

"At first I thought I wouldn't even be able to relate to her, but now I'm getting to like her."

"The crystals and the jewelry, the peasant blouse, the whole gypsy bit—don't you think it's a sign of bad brain fuzz?"

I laughed. " 'Brain fuzz.' . . . Yeah, I guess you could say she's got some of that, but she means well, and that's what counts."

"Interesting. Where's she from?"

"Well, I know she grew up in foster homes and group homes, and she's even lived on the street."

"You mean, like homeless?"

"That's the impression I get—I still don't know her very well. She's a mystery, really intriguing. She seems like one of those people you hear about who never bonded with anyone when they were young, and then they spend their lives drifting. You know, the people in this group . . . they're more interesting than I thought they'd be. They're not what I expected."

"You're much more relaxed than when you first got here. I remember watching you—"

"Back in base camp?"

"Sure. You didn't know what to expect. You thought

you were going to be attacked at any moment."

"I thought I didn't let on."

He smiled and winked. "I can tell these things. But you adapted fast. You have a lot of personal strength. But you're still afraid of Pug, aren't you?"

"I've never liked guys that are always flexing their muscles."

"Well, let me tell you the worst—he stabbed somebody."

"You're kidding!"

"He was raised by his stepfather, a really mean guy, I guess. Beat Pug and his little brother up all the time. That's why Pug's always looking for a shoulder to punch or somebody to sit on."

"I don't know how you can stand that, him punching you all the time. I think he's creepy."

"It's just a little ritual. Anyway a couple of years ago Pug put a knife in his stepfather. Lucky for Pug he didn't kill him—they would have put him away for sure."

"That's scary. Don't you think it's scary?"

Troy shook his head. "He's no danger to us. Guys like Pug don't have any *mental* toughness, and as long as you realize that you can stay way out in front of them."

I was impressed. "You know a lot about people."

"It's kind of a hobby."

"So what do you make of Heather and Rita?"

He smiled. "Heather's your classic nobody. Probably ran away a dozen times, doesn't have any idea what she's doing. Always trying to impress somebody. I'll bet anything her father's an alcoholic—like Adam's."

"You amaze me. You're incredibly perceptive."

"And Rita—I get a huge kick out of her, as long as she's not on my case. She's for real. She grew up with six brothers, no sisters. You know she actually ran a burglary ring in New York City? Had people bring her hot jewelry, TV's, stereos, and she would fence 'em herself."

"Who told you?"

"She did."

"She was bragging."

"Of course. But all the same, she was telling the truth. I can tell."

I hesitated, and then said, "What about Freddy?"

Troy hesitated too. He looked at me and cast around as if to find something, and then he said, "I can't get a fix on him—he doesn't talk to anybody. One thing I've figured out . . . you kind of like him, don't you?"

I was surprised. "Why do you say that?"

"Oh, just a hunch."

"I told him to get lost."

"Maybe you did, but that doesn't mean anything."

Confused, I looked away, then stopped in the trail. We looked each other in the eyes. Troy's deep, deep blue eyes were staring into mine with that same unblinking, soul-seizing look he'd fastened on me before. This time I didn't blink either, and I didn't look away. "I don't care about Freddy," I said.

It started to rain. We looked a little longer into each other's eyes, and then we finally took off our packs and broke out our rain gear. We walked another mile or so, quiet now, because we couldn't hear anything with our hoods up but the rain. We came upon the others huddled under the shaggy limbs of a big spruce, and this time they didn't say anything. They were standing around spouting jets of vapor, like horses.

Several steep miles below us, base camp came into sight and made a homey picture, with its little log cabins alongside the river. We weren't that far away from hot showers, a good hot meal, and rest. Al seized the optimism of the moment to walk alongside me and see if I was ready for some counseling. "How do you feel now, Jessie? Any better?"

"Not really," I said, even though I did. What was I going to say? Sure, Al, I'm feeling much better. Thank you very much for terrifying me out of my mind and almost killing me.

"I understand," he said. "It was scary. But Jessie, you have to believe in your own unlimited potential. I really believe that. Stretch yourself. Do something great. Dare to be great. Don't accept your limitations; outgrow them."

That did it. "Get lost, Al!" I screamed at him. "Get away from me, and take your condescending psycho-babble with you!"

Rita and Pug were howling, and Troy smiled approvingly at Al's confusion. I couldn't believe Al thought he could do that to me and get away with it. I'd heard all this back in Boulder a hundred times before. And they think you should have to take it just because you're a kid and they're the adults.

"Stretch yourself!" Adam repeated, marveling over the phrase like it was a work of art. *"Go stretch yourself."*

"You know what I'm talking about, Adam," Al said defensively.

"Sure. Stretching is torture and torture is good. Torture

is the way to enlightenment—ancient marine wisdom."

Pug's ears perked up. I could tell it was either torture or the marines that had him excited, probably both.

"Naw, let's not call it torture," Al said, the knowing grin returning to his face. "How about, 'wilderness therapy'?"

"Wil-der-ness ther-a-py," Adam chanted. "I like the sound of it. Lots of stretching involved in that 'wilderness therapy,' I bet."

Pug wasn't following closely. "I think we should fight the Vietnam War over again, and win it this time."

This wasn't the first time he'd pestered Al about Vietnam. He couldn't stand it that Al wasn't gung-ho, especially considering he'd actually been there and fought in combat.

"You'd have to kill most of the civilian population," Al said.

"Fine with me," Pug snorted. "Waste 'em all and let God sort 'em out."

· 4 ·

THE FIRST THING I DID WHEN WE GOT TO BASE camp was race into my cabin and look in the mirror. It was much worse than I'd even guessed. My hair was all plastered down, my face was a total mess. There was a big smudge on my cheek, where I'd touched my face, from the black that comes off the cooking pots. Star came in behind me and smiled as she saw me looking in the mirror. "I can't believe it," I said. "Tell me if I ever look this bad again, okay? I can't wait to get into the shower."

"Me too. Rita and Heather said to tell you that the guys are building the fire in the boiler, and they're planning on getting into the shower first."

"How unchivalrous! I mean, we've been out in the rain for a week and none of us complained about suffering along with the guys, but I really wouldn't mind a little inequality just once, like now, when it comes to the showers."

34

"That's what Rita and Heather thought. They said we'll sneak in right before them."

"All right! Are you with us?"

"Sure."

Star and I got our kindling fired up in the little potbelly stove, and started stoking it with wood we'd split and kept dry while we were gone, in anticipation of this moment. Pretty soon the cabin was toasty hot. Across from us, Heather had her cabin's chimney puffing, while Rita staked out the showerhouse. She watched as Pug came and went, restoking his fire in the boiler and testing the temperature of the water. After hollering "Almost!" to Adam, who was out in front of his cabin chopping wood, Pug disappeared into the cabin he shared with Troy. Freddy was nowhere around. At Rita's signal we sneaked around the back of the showerhouse. Each time Adam raised the axe over his head and concentrated on his target, one of us would dart inside, laden with clean clothes and towels and all the soap, shampoo, conditioners, and lotions we could carry.

The water was plenty hot. It was exquisitely hot. I don't think I ever felt so good in my whole life as I did letting it pound on my sore shoulders. We were all shrieking with the pure pleasure of it and the joyous sight of the week's grime heading for the drain. I shampooed again and again, I scrubbed and scrubbed, I let the hot water play all over my back. "Hot stuff!" Rita was hollering. "We're hot stuff! Mountain girls!"

The hot water was running out as we heard voices suddenly snickering in the changing room, and then the outside door banged, and Pug and Adam were whooping it up. We looked at each other, suddenly realizing our predicament, and Heather said, "Uh-oh."

"You guys give us those clothes back," Rita screamed, "or you're gonna be sorrier than sorry."

Pug was laughing his head off. I could picture him well enough, with all our clean stuff balled up in his huge, grimy grasp.

"What'll you give us for 'em?" Adam wanted to know.

By now I could hear Troy's laugh along with theirs. For a second I thought of appealing to him, but I knew I shouldn't.

"Give 'em back right now and we won't rip your faces off," Rita declared.

"You're going to have to do better than that. You girls have committed a heinous crime, and now you're going to have to pay!"

"State your terms," I shouted.

"Ah," Adam replied merrily, "the voice of reason. . . . Let's parley, mates."

They had their parley. It was a spirited debate. We could hear only snatches of it, and most of those I wouldn't care to repeat.

"Hurry up!" Heather wailed. "We're completely out of hot water . . . it's cold in here!"

"Too . . . bad. . . ."

"Ladies and gentlemen," Adam intoned, "the terms are as follows: It's Troy's and my turn to cook tonight. We return your stuff if Rita cooks that same lasagna she did before we went out on the hike."

"Deal!" Rita shouted. "Hey, I love to cook." Then she

turned to us and whispered, "You watch. Where I come from we don't get mad, we get even."

Back in our cabin, Star and I stoked the fire and sat with our backs to the stove, drying our hair. Mine dried first—it's shoulder length, and not as thick as Star's, either. I brushed Star's out for her, and as we talked, I found myself telling her how I'd been thinking about calling my father, but now I wasn't going to. "I can't believe he's marrying a lawyer," I said. "She seems so different from him. And she's a lot younger than he is—she's only thirty-four. My dad is forty-five."

Star didn't comment. I had the sudden insight that I was telling a homeless girl about my home.

"I was really scared up there, when I fell," I said.

"You were brave."

I laughed. "Sure."

"No, really, you went first, with Freddy. That peak was swirling with negative energy."

"It was, wasn't it? I felt like I got hit by a train. And could you believe Al, the line he was feeding me? After he almost got me killed?"

Star got up, took the crystal from the pendant around her neck, and offered it to me. "If you lie back, put this on your forehead, and think positive, your anger will leave you."

I set the brush aside. "Sure," I said with a little laugh, "why not?"

Star walked lightly as ever over to her bed. Her reddish-brown hair fell halfway to her waist. Freshly washed and brushed, it was beautiful. On her left hand and right ankle she wore those colorful woven "friendship bracelets."

I lay back on my bed with the crystal on my forehead, smiled a little to myself, and rested. Star brought out a small wooden box, the kind you might find in Mexico, from among her things. I'd never seen it before. One of her secrets. "What's in it?" I asked.

"The Royal Road of Tarot."

I sat up. "Tarot cards? I've heard of them, but I've never seen them."

"I thought you might be a person who is open to what the Tarot can offer."

"I need some kind of help. I feel like a wreck."

"Let's sit on the floor. The floor would be best."

"How come?"

"Wood enhances the spirit of the cards and shields them from negative vibrations. That's why I keep them in this wooden box."

We sat side by side on the floor. Star gently lifted the lid of the box and removed a silk-wrapped bundle.

"What pretty silk," I remarked, and touched it. It felt lovely.

"Silver for my soul color. Silver is the color of starlight."

"Did your parents name you 'Star'?"

"No," she said calmly. "I did."

I wasn't sure if I should press her to talk about her past, so I let the moment go, but I felt closer to her. She was right about her "soul color," I thought. Wispy silver, fragile and ethereal, like herself. I felt like it was an honor to have her pull out her cards for me and tell me about her soul color. I wondered why someone so gentle could have been left homeless. I wondered, too, about the horrible things I'd heard that happen to homeless girls on the streets. Could Star have been through things like that?

She unwound the silk wrapping from the cards and handed them to me. "Shuffle them," she said. As I was doing so, she spread a royal blue silk cloth out on the floor.

When I had shuffled them three times, she said that it was enough. She took a small notepad and pencil from the wooden box and handed them to me. "Write out your question," she said.

"Me? What question?"

"Whatever you want to know," Star said softly. "Or if you don't have a specific question, just write, 'Wisdom of the Tarot.' "

I felt a little strange. I wrote, 'Wisdom of the Tarot,' whatever that means.

"Concentrate on the paper, and the question will absorb the energy of the deck."

Star began to lay out the cards. "This is called the Celtic Cross. This first card, the Nine of Pentacles, helps me to understand your state of mind. This next card, the Magician, can be either good or bad. We'll need to see first how the other cards come up. The Four of Cups tells how your past is affecting you right now. The Five of Swords is your past. The King of Cups could come into your life. The Wheel—"

I was fascinated. "What are 'cups'?" I interrupted. "What are 'pentacles'?"

"Cups are like hearts in a regular deck of cards. But wait—we have to finish laying out all ten before we can interpret. Close your eyes, Jessie, and tune in to your higher self. Let your inner eye see the cards. Now, the seventh card . . . the Wheel of Fortune represents your negative feelings. The Sun represents the feelings of those around you. The King of Cups represents your own positive feelings, and the Eight of Cups is the outcome."

"Can I open my eyes?"

"Sure."

The cards were pretty to look at, exotic human figures and strange symbols. "Well?" I asked expectantly.

Star smiled. "Lots of cups, Jessie."

"So what are 'cups'?"

"Love and happiness. Like hearts, remember?"

"Oh, good. Tell me more."

"Five out of ten cards are cups. That's pretty unusual. Love and happiness, then, is the center of your reading."

"Is that all?"

"Except that the King of Cups here is in the reverse position. That means you are open to a new relationship."

"Sounds good to me," I giggled. "The King of Hearts. Think it could be anybody we know?"

The dinner gong was sounding. That meant we had to get to the dining hall quickly, or Pug would eat all the food. "Quick," I said. "Let's go."

I was pulling on my sweater and was halfway out the door. Star was still sitting cross-legged on the floor, looking perplexed that I'd want to run out in the middle of our reading. "I'm starving," I explained. "Is there something more?"

"Your wish will not come to fulfillment at this time."

"Darn!" I said. "C'mon, Star, let's eat."

We ran over to the dining hall. Rita was serving her

lasagna buffet-style. She'd baked it in two casserole dishes, and as she set them out at some distance from each other, she shouted that the smaller one was for the girls and the larger one for the guys.

"How considerate," Adam said, in a mock British accent.

First in line, Pug was delighted, and dished up even more for himself than usual.

We served ourselves and sat down at the big table. Freddy was back. I noticed him glancing at me, just a glance, and when he saw me notice him he looked away. The place was buzzing. A genuine hot meal, and everyone knew in advance it was going to be world-class.

As Troy sat down next to me, he said, "Feeling good?"

"I sure am," I said. "I feel great."

"Good."

I took a bite of Rita's lasagna. It was delicious. I felt warm and good. I thought about my Tarot reading and smiled to myself. I wondered how Troy fit into my "love and happiness." I might be open to a new relationship—the cards were right about that. The cards must always be right, I thought, like fortune cookies. Really they could apply to anything. But I wouldn't tell Star how skeptical I was. The cards were fun, anyway, and gave you a lot to think about. What *about* Troy? I wondered. Was he the King of Hearts?

All of a sudden, there was pandemonium. Troy was gagging, and so was Adam. Pug was shoveling the lasagna down so fast, he hadn't realized there was a problem, but now he did—he spit out what was in his mouth.

Adam said, "Try a little garlic next time, Rita."

Rita sprang to her feet and raised a fist in triumph. *"Gotcha!"*

"Got me too," Al muttered.

I tried a little bit of Troy's lasagna. It was unbelievable. A half-dozen garlic bulbs—not cloves—must've gone into the guys' casserole. The one for the girls tasted just great.

Al didn't look too happy. He was hungry. But what was he going to do about it?

"Check out Freddy," Pug said.

Freddy was eating away like nothing was wrong. His plateful of lasagna was half gone.

Heather tried a bit of his, and said, " 'Try a little garlic' is right. How can you eat that?"

He shrugged, and flashed his smile. He had the most beautiful teeth. "Pretty good. Kills worms, too, I bet."

Everybody laughed, and the way it ended up, it turned into a macho contest. The guys cleaned their plates, even Al. Adam was going around to each of the girls with his lips out like a goldfish, saying, "Give us a kiss, give us a kiss."

After dinner we were supposed to be making plans for running the San Juan River. The girls were off to one side, keeping their distance from the garlic victims. Everybody was complaining that there wouldn't be any rapids on the San Juan. "We all want to do a whitewater river, Al," I said.

"I've been looking into that," Al said, with a grin.

"And? . . ." asked Troy.

"It's hard to find whitewater this late in the year," Al explained, "but with the recent rains, the Colorado River is running high in Westwater Canyon, below Grand Junction and just across the Utah line. Ten thousand cubic feet per second—I called and checked. That's a great level for Westwater. Before we do our long trip on the San Juan, we can train on some prime whitewater on the Colorado.

Westwater is a one-day stretch, but we could camp there for three or four days and just keep running it over and over."

"Is is very . . . rough?" Heather asked.

"There's a rapid in there that, at some water levels, is rated a ten on a ten-scale. It's called Skull, and it can be just as nasty as Crystal or Lava Falls."

"I've heard those names," said Troy. "They're in the Grand Canyon."

"So why don't we just run the Grand Canyon?" Rita shouted. "We'll kick its butt."

"Yeah, right," Al said with an appreciative smile. "Well, among other considerations, we can't get a permit for the Grand, but we can pick one up for Westwater on the spot. I promise it'll knock your socks off."

Adam couldn't help himself. In a perfect mother impersonation, he said, "Bring lots of extra socks, everybody."

·5·

AL HAD BEEN RIGHT ABOUT WESTWATER. IT knocked our socks off. We were still talking about it as we approached the San Juan River. Al was driving slowly because we were pulling the heavy trailer with gear for a ten-day float. We were suffering from white water withdrawal. "Skull was awesome," Adam was saying. "I'll never forget it. Especially the look on everybody's face when we dropped into the hole."

"I was too busy paddling to notice," Rita shouted. "Maybe if Redhead here was paddling instead of messing around, we wouldn't have gone into the hole. Al missed it by a mile with his raft."

"Your mother . . . ," Adam teased.

Rita reached out and grabbed Adam's T-shirt by the neck, and pulled him toward her. "—wears ordinary women's shoes, and if you say anything different . . ."

"Al was rowing, not paddling," Troy said. "You have

more control with those oars than with a bunch of paddles."

"The part I liked best," Adam said merrily, "was the Room of Doom. We almost got sucked in there the first day. Around and around you go, *and you can't get out.* That would've been interesting—floating around all day with that dead cow."

Pug was chortling. "The part I liked best was when Heather went flying, like she was shot out of a gun. And the look on her face when she was suddenly out in the river."

Riding shotgun in the van, Heather rolled her head and groaned. It wasn't a pleasant memory, I'm sure. When we dropped into that hole in Skull Rapid, in Westwater Canyon, the boat folded like a sandwich made from one slice of bread. Everybody crashed into each other, and when the boat sprang back to its normal length, it catapulted her out just the way Pug said, as if she'd been shot from a cannon. But that wasn't the worst part. She was caught in the hole, and the white water recirculated her over and over before spitting her out. It must have felt like she was in a cross between a washing machine and a garbage disposal.

Once Heather was rescued, she lost it, got really hysterical. It wasn't pretty to watch. Star and I helped settle her down. After that, the fear never left her eyes. That happened on our first day on Westwater, and then she wouldn't get back on the water for our second and third runs, no matter how much Al counseled her about "getting back on the horse." She stayed by the van and waited for us.

After our last run through Westwater Canyon, we spent a couple of hours loading the boats with all the overnight gear we'd need for three more days of flat floating downstream, all the way to Moab, Utah. Heather got back on board after Al promised it would all be flat. It was. Pretty in stretches, with red cliffs along the river and snow-covered mountains in the background, but it wasn't whitewater.

The van rumbled from Colorado into Utah, and we passed through the little towns of Monticello and Blanding. We were nearing the San Juan. It had taken days of work and preparation back in base camp—shopping from Al's shopping lists, packing waterproof metal "rocket boxes" with a ten-day supply of food, stuffing all our personal gear into huge waterproof bags—and we were exhausted. We'd chattered for hours about Westwater and whatever else came up, but the long drive had finally worn us down, and most people had nodded off. Troy's head was on my shoulder, and I wasn't very comfortable, but I was happy. Only Freddy and I were awake. Freddy, as ever, was studying the countryside like it was the most interesting thing in the world.

I looked around at the barren high desert of southeast Utah. I'd never been out this way with my dad. It didn't look very interesting to me until we drove into Bluff, a tiny town with old buildings made out of blocks of red stone. The huge cottonwoods that lined the road wore their fall colors, and it was warm. We stopped at a gas station and convenience store. It would be our last stop. The put-in for the San Juan River was only three miles away.

"Last chance for junk food," Adam said with a crazed look, as he slapped himself into consciousness. "Let's go in there and clean 'em out."

Pug took him seriously. "Ten days on the river is a long time. . . ."

"It's gonna get grim out there," Adam added. "People are gonna kill for a little bag of chips."

Pug counted out his available funds. Freddy and Star wandered by him, looking around aimlessly. They never had any money. I'd tried loaning Star some, but there wasn't much she wanted from the material world.

Mildly irritated, Al raised his voice. "Keep in mind, we have three meals a day packed in the rocket boxes on the trailer. Nobody's gonna starve."

"Tell you what," Troy said suddenly. "Pick out whatever you want, everybody—I can cover it."

Pug's mouth fell open. "You're kiddin'."

We were all pretty astonished, including Al and the guy at the cash register.

Troy shrugged. "I'm serious. That's what money's for, isn't it? Anything in the store you want." Then he flashed his golden smile, and said, "No big deal."

It was interesting to see how people reacted. As happy as a kid on Christmas morning, Pug had his arms so full he was dropping stuff. The clerk gave him a bag. Adam accompanied Pug around the store for the fun of it, encouraging him to take this and that. At the magazine rack, they picked out *Soldier of Fortune* for Pug, and Adam got a couple of Ninja magazines for himself. He struck a few martial arts poses and went around the store grunting in mock Japanese. I had to laugh, remembering about his moonlit escapades on the rooftops, the roses on the pillows.

Rita was on a shopping jag, too. I was just watching.

"C'mon, Jessie," Troy encouraged me. "It's our last chance. You know, ten days in the wilderness and all that."

"Are you sure? It's going to be a lot." I nodded toward the big hitters.

"No problem. My treat. Star, Heather, Freddy . . . if we're going to have a good time on the river, we're going to need some supplies."

I picked out a little junk food, but Star refrained. She was so conscious about what she ate, her body was practically translucent. Not that she was anorexic—Star would eat, as long as it was natural food and no red meat. She and I picked out some lotions and lip stuff, and I talked her into a pair of sunglasses with some colorful loops to hold them on.

It was a windfall for the fellow at the counter. Troy never flinched, either. I'd never met anyone that generous before. Heather thanked him, and he said, "For my friends . . ." Freddy was kind of disappearing out the door when Troy said, "Freddy, isn't there anything?"

There was a tone in Troy's voice, like his feelings were about to be hurt. I knew he was intrigued with Freddy—he'd never met anyone like him before. None of us really knew who Freddy was.

Freddy glanced back at Troy, and he smiled his bright, shy smile. "Sure," he said. "Thanks." He picked out a Hershey bar and a Coke, and that was it.

It was dusk. Al drove us to the edge of town, and we stopped at an old stone garage with a half-inflated raft out front and a huge sign that said, "SCENIC SAN JUAN RIVER TRIPS."

Al turned around and said, "This should only take a few

minutes. They're shut down for the season, but they're going to do our shuttle for us—drive the van and trailer to the end of the line while we're on the river."

It wasn't a few minutes. Apparently Al was having trouble with his shuttle arrangements.

We were having a good time in the van, munching on junk food and visiting. The talk turned to the San Juan. What was it going to be like? Pretty boring, was the consensus, after our wild adventures on the Colorado in Westwater Canyon.

Adam's voice turned lunatic. "Give me whitewater, I say. Give me *white* water!"

"So we're supposed to do ten days on a flat river," Troy said. "And you know why?"

"Yeah," Rita blurted, "Because Al said that's where he could get a permit."

"That's right. That's the only reason. But that's pretty lame, if you think about it. Why should *Hoods in the Woods* need a permit?"

Adam laughed. "That's about like bank robbers applying for a loan."

"It's Al who needs the permit, not us. We can go anywhere we want!"

"Vegas," Adam said, just that fast.

Rita was shaking her head. "Gotta be L.A."

"Miami," Pug insisted.

"I'm serious," Troy said. "The keys are in the ignition."

Our attention was immediately riveted to those keys and the sudden significance that Troy had given them. The van crackled with energy. With one stroke Troy had turned our imaginations up to white-hot. It was a priceless moment.

Rita and Pug were going wild and Adam was slapping Troy on the back. I checked Freddy out; he was amused. Heather was awfully quiet, with a nervous little smile on her face. But if she'd said anything, Rita would have ripped her face off.

Troy looked around the van, to each of us, and settled us down with the power of his eyes.

"We can go anywhere we want," I said softly, trying out the idea.

I thought how my dad would feel. He'd find out it wasn't going to be as tidy as he thought to ship me off to a "program," where he could picture me in a certain box. He'd have to account for my feelings for a change.

"Where to?" Rita said impatiently. "Hey, I could show you guys around New York."

Troy was shaking his head. "That's what they'd expect us to do. And think about how fast they'd pick us up."

"We could steal a different car," Pug offered.

"Okay, everybody, now think about that trailer we're pulling. It's got two boats' worth of gear and a ten-day supply of food. I'm thinking, if we could get off the roads and get on to a river—not this one—we could slip away and have ourselves a good time."

There was plenty of noisy agreement about that.

"Hang in there," Troy said, and we hushed up. "The question is, can we launch before they catch us? They'd never guess we're on a river, let alone which one. And it's October—there won't hardly be anyone on the river but us, just like it was at Westwater."

"Rhaat onnnn!" Pug thundered.

We all knew Troy was about to name the river, but

DOWNRIVER

nobody had the slightest idea what it might be. "Hurry," Rita said, "Al could come out any minute!"

"Easy," Troy assured her. "Remember, everybody . . . remember how Al said Skull was a 'Grand Canyon–class rapid'? You remember that?"

"Sure, sure," we answered.

"Well, we did fine in Skull. Heather took a swim, but big deal. And it was a blast. *So why don't we run the Grand Canyon?*"

There followed several moments of total silence, a rare event for the eight of us. It was an awesome thought, outrageous and inspired. There was a beauty to the idea, grand, wild, and majestic, drawing power and mystery from the canyon itself. You'd have to be awfully nervy to think you could up and run the Grand Canyon, as inexperienced as we were. No adults, just us.

The calm broke into a babble of excited voices.

"We could do it!" Adam cheered.

"Ten days of food," Troy added, "and all the rafting gear's packed on the trailer."

"Could we really do it?" I asked Troy. "Would we make it through?"

"Like Adam said, we were awesome in Westwater. It sure would be fun trying."

A thrill of fear went through me. "Do we even know where to start?"

"Sure. Lee's Ferry, Arizona. Remember, Al mentioned that's where all the Grand Canyon trips start."

"We should have Al with us," Heather put in nervously. "Hasn't he been down the Grand Canyon four times?"

Rita put her face in Heather's. "Are you out of your

51

mind? No permit, get it? You can't go legal. You think Al's going to help us sneak it? Forget Al—we'll have a lot more fun without him."

Heather was trying to catch her breath. "But isn't it some kind of crime? What would they do to us?"

Suddenly I could see myself in a cell, and just that fast I felt all queasy. I'd been in trouble before, but never in *jail*.

Everybody was quiet, and looking to Troy.

He shrugged. "Some kind of larceny, wouldn't it be? I can't expect we'd serve life in prison for moving Al's van a coupla hundred miles and then taking his gear downstream. It'll be obvious we didn't intend to *steal* any of it."

Adam broke a long moment of tense silence as he shouted, "Hey, wait a minute! This is perfect. Troy's last name is 'Larsen,' right? This will be a case of *'Grand Larsen-y'!"*

Everybody groaned, and Pug pounded Adam on the shoulder, then a few more times for good measure.

"Put him out of his misery," jeered Rita.

Adam was mugging only a bit sheepishly. "Get it, Rita? Are you *sure* you got it?"

"Look," Troy said, eyeing the door of the office next to the garage. "Al's going to come out of there in a minute and then this will have been just another bull session." He looked us over again, with blue eyes blazing, taking our measure, and when he got to Freddy, he stopped and stared at him.

"Freddy," Troy said finally. "What do you think, Freddy? We haven't heard from you."

The way he said it, and especially considering the timing,

I got the idea it all hinged on Freddy, somehow. It seemed improbable, but true.

Freddy shrugged. "For me, it would be worth it. The *Grand Canyon?* Sure. You bet."

"Good deal," Troy said.

Freddy, who was in the very back seat, leaned forward. "We have to make it to the river first. Cops'll be looking for us up ahead, after Al puts out the word. But I know some back roads through the reservation. . . ."

Pug, who'd always seemed to dislike Freddy, roared his approval.

Is this really happening? I thought. We aren't just talking about it?

Troy slid up to the driver's seat and had Freddy trade out for Heather up front. He put his fingers on the keys and said, "It's an adventure. Take us to Lee's Ferry, Freddy."

Rita reached forward and grabbed Troy's shoulder. "So what makes you think they won't catch us there, smart guy?"

Troy turned around and gave us a sly smile. "In the middle of the night?"

· 6 ·

WE DROVE OUT SO SLOWLY AND QUIETLY, AL never even came to the door of the shop. Within a few minutes we'd crossed the muddy San Juan and passed the sign that said we were entering the Navajo Nation. The mood inside the van was delirious—an intoxicating combination of excitement and fear. Troy had his foot down on the gas pedal, trying to get off the main road as quickly as we could. Up ahead dozens of gigantic red formations were catching the last of the sunset. "Check it out," Rita crowed. "It's like office buildings made of stone."

"Monument Valley," Freddy said. "Here's that side road. Turn at the trading post."

Pug's face was practically propped on Troy's shoulder. "Let's get some booze and cigarettes," he said. "I can pass for twenty-one."

Troy drove right on by the trading post and onto the gravel road. "If we stop, they're going to pick up on us and we'll have cops on our tail real quick."

"He's right," Freddy said. "Besides, they don't even sell liquor on the reservation."

"Wise guy," Pug said. "Anybody got any cigarettes?"

Troy ran his hand through his hair. "Hey, Big Fella, we're in great shape. We're off the highway, it's going to be dark soon, and both tanks are full of gas. But if we make any stops, we're going to blow it."

"Yeah, yeah, I'm cool if you are. Hey, Freddy, is that really your name?"

"Federico."

I wondered why Pug seemed to dislike Freddy. The way Pug looked at him made me wonder if it was Freddy's dark skin.

"How come you don't go by 'Rico' then?"

Freddy's eyes flashed. I had the feeling he wasn't afraid of anybody, including Pug. "'Cause my name's Freddy," he said.

Pug's face returned to Troy's shoulder once again. "Need a break driving, buddy?"

"No thanks, Pug, I can drive all night. Driven cross-country lots of times."

Star was sitting next to me. She whispered, "Can we really run the Grand Canyon, Jessie?"

"That's exactly what I've been wondering," I whispered back. "I sure hope so. I'm pretty scared, to tell you the truth. Are you scared?"

"You shouldn't even talk like that. It's negative thinking. You can make something bad happen, if you image it."

"I don't even know what it'll be like, so how can I image it?"

"We could ask the Tarot."

"How about right now?"

"Oh no," she said softly. "Too many influences on the cards. It wouldn't be right in here."

"So you're going to start down the Grand Canyon without knowing what it would say?"

Her green eyes were calm—maybe too calm to be real, I thought.

"I'm a water sign," Star said. "A Pisces. A fish can always swim."

A couple of hours passed as we rumbled down the backroads. Everyone in the back was nodding off, even Rita. I was exhausted, and slept in fits and starts. Once, I woke up, looked around, and saw only Freddy and Troy awake up front. They were talking quietly, actually communicating with each other. I thought that was a good sign. Our lives were going to depend on those two guys.

I noticed Troy checking me out in the rear-view mirror. The whites showed all around his eyes. Our driver was totally alert, as advertised. He gave me a thumbs-up.

I felt good all down my spine. I felt alive. This was going to be an adventure, all right. I didn't go back to sleep, I was too excited. I thought about my dad, how this was much more than he'd bargained for. It would be the ultimate way to show him. Al, too. They both deserved it.

We rumbled on into the night, occasionally passing by sleeping Navajo hogans and deserted roadside jewelry stands, and the sense of the isolation into which we were plunging got me to imagining more and more what it might be like to actually be in the Grand Canyon, beyond any help and trying to make it through alive. I could picture only the vaguest of shapes; the place loomed impossibly huge, mythical, ominous. I remembered the thrashing Heather took in Skull rapid. Al said that Skull was an 8 on a 10-scale at the level we ran it. What must a 9 or a 10 look like? What would happen to us down there?

Brooding more with every passing mile, I actually began to hope that we'd have a flat or that the van would break down. But it kept rumbling along. We passed a gas station in the middle of nowhere, closed down for the night, and I realized I'd seen a phone booth. Panicky, I leaned forward and touched Troy on the shoulder. "Stop," I said.

He looked over his shoulder at me, confused and unwilling.

"Stop!" I yelled. If anybody had been asleep, they were awake now.

Troy brought the van to a stop on the side of the road. "What is it?"

I was practically desperate. I didn't care what anybody thought. "I have to make a phone call," I said.

"You're kidding," Pug said. He looked around. "She thought she'd make a phone call."

I was backing out the side door. Everyone's eyes were on me. I just kept going, got outside and started running back toward the gas station.

Troy caught up with me as I ran. "What're you doing?"

"Making a phone call."

"Who are you calling?"

"My father."

He looked sick. He didn't say anything. He just kept jogging.

"Don't worry. I won't say where we are or where we're going. I just have to talk to him, okay?"

When I got there, Troy stood only about fifteen feet away from the booth. I went inside, shut the door, and turned my back to him. I was breathing hard as I asked the operator to make the call collect. I was afraid Madeline would answer. I was so panicky, I didn't know what I would do if she answered.

My father answered. "Jessie, is that you? Where are you?"

I felt so confused. Now what was I going to do? Why was I calling him?

"That's not important," I said, still breathing hard, and my heart going wild.

"Jessie, are you all right?"

Troy, I realized, was standing right by the phone booth.

"Sure."

"You don't sound so good. Is anything wrong?"

"No, nothing's wrong. . . ."

"Where are you calling from?"

Somehow he knew I wasn't where I was supposed to be. What was it I wanted to tell him?

"Look, Dad . . . we're going to do something, okay?"

"Jessie, talk to me. You can talk to me. What is it you're going to do?"

I looked up into Troy's face. He was pretty unhappy, and he was signaling with his finger across the throat. I wasn't answering my dad. I was so confused.

"Jessie, I have confidence in you. I know you'll do the right thing. Don't make any choices you won't want to live with, okay?"

"Sure, Dad," I sniffled. I wanted to speak, but I couldn't. I wanted to say "I love you." I felt like it might be the last chance, but I didn't. I don't know if I couldn't, I only know I didn't.

"Jessie . . ."

"I'll be okay, Dad. *Bye.*" Quickly I hung up the phone.

Troy and I didn't talk about it. And I was too disoriented, too guilty, even to think about how pushy Troy had been. When I got back in the van, Rita said, with those beady black eyes, "So, who'd you call?"

"My father, all right?"

"Jessie didn't say anything," Troy explained as he started up the van.

"So I coulda called my mother," Rita wailed. "You guys are really considerate, you know that?"

Adam laughed and said, "Notice who didn't leave the keys in the ignition."

"Well, I feel a lot better," I said.

"How nice for you," Heather snapped.

About one in the morning, Troy pulled out onto a narrow bridge and slowed the van down. "Colorado River!" he sang out, and we all came lurching out of our sleep and looked down. Far below, the black surface of the river was reflecting starlight. *Spooky.*

Past the bridge we came to a filling station and trading post that was all closed down for the night. "No more phone calls," Troy announced decisively. Pug said we should break in for "supplies," but everybody knew he was only talking. We turned down the road marked "LEE'S FERRY." After a couple of miles, we passed some parking lots, a campground, and a ranger station. The road dead-ended at a wide concrete boat ramp at the river. There were a couple of cars in the lot there, some bathrooms, and good overhead light.

"Nobody's around," Troy said. "Perfect. Okay, you guys, we know how to rig, just like we did at Westwater. Pump up the boats, rig frames, stow all the rocket boxes and dry bags, tie everything down. Dry bags in between the nets in the middle of the paddle raft, everything else on the oared raft. And *whisper*. Let's see how fast we can get out of here and slide downstream."

Pug hadn't been listening. Pointing over at a sign, he said, "Get a load of this: 'PRIVATE BOATERS MUST REGISTER PERMIT WITH THE RIVER RANGER.' What a laugh. Anybody see any river rangers?"

We set to work. We rigged the boats. We were out of our minds with anticipation. Were we really going to do this? We weren't just talking about it?

Troy drove the van and the trailer into a dirt lot, then came back. We were dead tired. The first hint of dawn was starting to show, and still no river rangers, nobody at all.

"We gotta get out of here," Troy said.

We hustled. It was all a blur, but finally the boats were rigged.

"Hey, where's Heather?" Rita said suddenly, and she wasn't whispering.

Everybody looked around, and the realization sunk in. "She split!" Rita said. "Heather split!"

Of course, I thought. It makes perfect sense.

"Run up to the john," Troy ordered. "Check both of 'em."

Adam and Rita came running back. "Gone," they said, breathing hard. "What do we do?"

"Yeah," Pug said, "what if she squeals?"

Troy reached for his life jacket. "Forget it. So she squeals."

We moved toward the boats. One was a paddle raft, with all of our personal stuff in the dry bags, and one was the rowed raft with all the food and group gear. "Who's rowing?" I asked. Al had rowed on the Westwater trip.

"I am," Troy answered. "Let's get going!"

"You got a river map, Troy?" Freddy asked.

Troy waved his arms impatiently. His eyes were jumpy; I'd never seen him nervous like this before. "I got my Arizona road map," he said. "It's got the river on it."

He didn't say it like a joke, that was the thing. Adam didn't even make hay out of it, and he'd never been handed a better setup. This was the moment. We could've backed out right there. We all looked around at each other, and I bet we were all thinking the same thing. We didn't really know what we were doing, yet we'd dared each other into this. If we backed down now, our self-respect was going to go down the tubes. We'd be totally whipped.

Of all people, I grabbed my paddle and stepped into the paddle raft. Maybe I wanted to make up for the phone call, or for being the one who kept us from the top of Storm King Peak. "We'll make it up as we go," I said. "We can't get lost—you just float downriver!"

Star was right behind me. "I'm with Jessie," she said.

Troy was pleased. "We can scout the rapids as we come to 'em. Remember how good we were in Westwater."

"I want muh mother," Pug sang, and everybody laughed.

And then we were off, paddling for the current in the dawn, the ramp slipping away behind us. We paddled through a riffle, alongside a low cliff on the left, and passed into the rising walls of a canyon. With a look back I saw the water tower at the ranger station disappear. Troy rowed his boat alongside ours. Barely above us, bats were zooming at crazy angles. "Let's put that bridge behind us before we stop," Troy advised. "Well, guys, we're really doing it, we're pirating the Grand Canyon of the Colorado."

"Pirates o' the Colorado!" Pug roared. He pulled out his buck knife—an item Al never knew about—and put it between his teeth.

"Ninja Pirates!" Adam declared.

Rita bounced up and down on the front of the raft. "Bring on the Grand Canyon—we'll kick its butt!"

And there was Freddy with a beautiful grin on his quiet face, his eyes drinking in the water, the walls, the bats, and the last reluctant stars.

◦ 7 ◦

WE PASSED UNDER THE BRIDGE, A GRACEFUL
arch composed of hundreds of steel girders, towering above
us in this world of stone and sky like a monumental work
of art. There was an eerie quality about it, as if it were the
vestige of an ancient civilization. No vehicles crossed it, no
one stood at the rail and waved to us. The river tugged at
us, and we bobbed along downstream. The bridge was
receding, and the sight sent a thrill down my spine. Ahead,
only rock, water, sky, and the unknown. In the next instant,
the thrill turned to fear, and I wished myself up on that
bridge looking down. What was I doing? Was I out of
my mind?

The canyon walls echoed the passage of a big truck. We
all looked back. It was a beer truck.

"Wish I had a rocket launcher," Pug said wistfully.

"Darn," Adam said. "I knew we forgot something."

"I'd blast that truck right off the bridge and watch it fall

all the way down to the river. Wouldn't that be a beautiful sight?"

It was touching to see Pug so affected by beauty.

"We'd be pickin' up beer all the way down the canyon," Rita said.

The current swept us around a little bend in the river, and the bridge was lost from view. It may as well have been hundreds of miles behind us.

From somewhere along the shore came the most delightful bird song I'd ever heard in my life, a series of lyrical whistles cascading in pitch and slowing as they fell. Star and I looked to each other. It was one of those moments you share with somebody, moments you never forget. She was so happy. Those green eyes were singing their own song.

There the song came again, and again. "I wish I knew its name," I said.

"Canyon wren," Freddy volunteered.

"How do you know?" Pug asked.

Freddy didn't bother to answer, just paddled on, with his eyes on the cliffs high above. It was almost as if he were reading lines in a book, his concentration was so focused. A mile or so later, he cocked one ear downstream, and then the other. I couldn't tell what he was hearing. Just then Troy yelled over from his boat, "What's that sound?"

Troy seemed kind of spooked; I still couldn't hear anything.

"Listen," he said. "Listen."

There was a background hum, or a vibration or something, coming from downstream.

"An airplane," Pug guessed.

I glanced at Freddy and saw a quiet smile on his face.

DOWNRIVER

"Tape hiss," Adam declared. "Canyon tape hiss."

Then it dawned on everybody at once. First rapid, of course. This was a whitewater river, after all.

We rounded a bend, and the sound wasn't so subtle. "Tape roar is more like it," I said.

"River Thunder," Adam named it. "Prepare to die, funhogs."

About three hundred yards downstream, the river seemed to end on its own horizon line. Past that spot the river wasn't visible at all. It looked like we were approaching a waterfall. The current almost died out, and we had to paddle downstream toward that brink as if we were on a lake. The River Thunder grew louder and louder.

We scouted the rapid—thank goodness we scouted it. We didn't know what it was called; its name wasn't on our Arizona road map. We didn't know how bad it was supposed to be, or how we were supposed to run it. I know how it looked: awful. It was all full of whitewater and studded with rocks, as the river narrowed and took a big fall. The main current led into waves bigger than any we'd seen in Westwater Canyon, but it seemed like the only way through was to go right into the big waves. To either side were boulders sticking up, and underneath them violent holes.

Everybody was standing around pointing, shouting to be heard over the roar of the rapid. I was right next to Freddy. "How'd all those boulders get in the river?" I asked him. "Did they fall off the cliffs?"

Freddy pointed out two side canyons, one entering the rapid on each side of the river. "I think they were washed out of those canyons. Flash floods."

I was amazed. The side canyons were bone dry. To think they could run with so much water as to carry down boulders as big as cars, and deposit them way out in the river. . . .

As we silently walked back to the boats, I felt the drums of doom in my ears. I looked upstream and wondered if we should give it all up. I thought about yelling out, calling for a conference.

I said nothing. Mechanically I picked up my paddle as Star picked up hers. She was sort of looking to me for reassurance. Just down the shore Troy was stowing his bowline; then he nudged his boat offshore and started rowing for the current. Star and I hugged each other, then laughed nervously at the odd feel of bumping life jackets. Adam, I could see, was thinking of poking a little fun, but he was too nervous.

"Let's get with it, kiddies," Troy called. "You gotta save me if I flip."

"I wish he wouldn't say that," Star fretted.

"Let's go!" Rita yelled. "Quit making such a big deal of this."

With our hearts jumping, we paddled out into the current, then slowly drifted toward the spot along the brink we'd picked. Ahead of us, Troy went over the edge and quickly disappeared. It was a heart-stopping sight.

Then it was our turn.

We picked up speed as the current flowed down the tongue. Into the valley of death, I thought, rowed the six hundred. And then we were into a churning fury of white water. Suddenly sideways in the big waves, the boat felt so unstable I thought we might tip over. I glanced to the very

back of the boat, to see if Pug was ruddering with his paddle. He didn't seem to know what he was doing. In fact he was doing the opposite of what he should have been and was causing us to get sideways.

Fool's luck: The rapid spit us out. We rode through the tailwaves, and then we were looking back up at the rapid, which looked like a staircase of white water. We were all cheering as we paddled our boat toward Troy's, and the canyon walls echoed Pug's war whoops. Troy was doing a victory dance atop the cooler, toward the front of his boat. "We can do this!" Troy yelled. "Perfect run! I hardly have any water to bail!" For the laid-back guy that he was, it was a major demonstration, and psyched us up still higher than we already were. Pug followed his captain's lead and started dancing on the gear in the middle of our boat, until Rita yelled, "Hey, that's our dry bags, you rhino! You're going to crush all our stuff!"

Pug looked bewildered, like a little boy chastised when he thought he was doing good. "Crush what? Like what?"

"Cookies?" Adam suggested hopefully.

Rita was standing up and had her hands on her hips. "Whaddaya want, a list of what's in everybody's dry bag? For pete's sake."

Pug slowly got off the gear. Confused, he didn't know whether to attack or apologize.

"Hey, guys," Troy said. "Remember, we're all in this together, and we're awesome."

"Right on!" Pug agreed.

The day was warming up. At last we were in the direct sunshine. Even though it was October, it was plenty warm, at least on those bends of the river that took the direct sun.

Troy took off his shirt and started working on his tan. The rest of the guys followed suit.

We landed for a pit stop. I found Troy and whispered to him about Pug, how he almost flipped us. "Maybe you should teach him," I suggested, "or else somebody else can be the rudder." Troy called Adam and Freddy over to talk, and I walked away. The guys were awfully macho about the rudder position. They assumed that none of the girls was strong enough to apply the torque necessary for a radical steering maneuver. Maybe *I* was, I thought, and Rita too. Heather for sure, with her wide shoulders, if she weren't so afraid. It was almost a shock to realize Heather was no longer among us. A few hours downstream, and we might as well have known her in another lifetime. She'd stayed behind, and we'd entered a separate reality.

Before we got back on the boats, Troy called us all together. With a little stick he drew diagrams in the wet sand and calmly talked abstract strategy, nothing about how we actually did in that first rapid.

Pug was taking it okay. He wasn't being singled out. The only problem was, when it came to the ruddering part, Troy's advice was so complicated I could barely follow it myself. I saw Pug nodding his head, but I had my doubts. Paddling is so instinctive: You're reacting to ever-changing conditions, and you do things with your paddle without really thinking about it.

When we got up and headed for the boats, I was sure everybody was thinking about who should rudder the paddle raft. Either Adam or Freddy would've been fine with me. They were great in Westwater. But as we were putting on our life jackets, Pug snatched up his paddle and practi-

cally jumped into the back of the boat. He had an awkward smile on his face. He knew we didn't trust him, but at the same time he couldn't help trying to prove himself.

Around the bend, more River Thunder. Another mile or two down we scouted another rapid as big as the first. Maybe the waves were even taller. "Are you going to take him off the rudder?" I whispered to Troy.

"Let's see what happens."

What happened was the same thing as before. Only this time, when we went up onto a big wave sideways, I got thrown out. One instant I was paddling, trying to do what I could to straighten the boat, and the next I was suddenly in that freezing green and white water. It was an overwhelming shock to find myself outside the boat and in the river. It could have been a whole lot worse, though. Fortunately, as I was flying out I'd grabbed the chicken line that ran around the boat and was holding on for dear life. I was only out for a few seconds, as it turned out. Star, of all people, did exactly what Al had taught us to do. She reached over my back and grabbed the bottom of my life jacket in one hand, the shoulder of my jacket with the other, and pulled me back into the boat like a tuna fisherman pulling a big one out of the sea.

We were both on the bottom of the front part of the boat, with our faces real close. Star was as surprised as I was. As the boat wallowed in the big waves I heard Freddy yell, "Adam—get in the back and rudder!" In the thick of that rapid, Freddy wasn't going to dance around Pug's feelings.

Adam brought us through the tailwaves rightside up. Freddy said, "Good work, Jessie. You hung on to your paddle."

Sure enough, there it was in my hand.

I glanced at Pug. His feelings were hurt, all right. And I didn't care. He was glaring at Freddy like he wanted to strangle him.

We bailed the boats out beneath the rapid, then had lunch on a long beach of pure white sand. I was sitting off by myself, on a big rock, trying to settle down. I was pretty shaken up after being in the river. It gave me pause to wonder what Heather went through when she was held under in the big hole in Skull and tumbled around and around. No wonder she bailed out on us. Was she the only one who knew what it was all about?

Troy came over and sat with me. "All's well that ends well," he said.

"Pug doesn't know what he's doing."

"I know. He's in a funk too. He knows he's out of that rudder spot, but I'd much rather have him feel bad about it than have him back there again."

"That's for sure."

"It looks like he's just gonna blame Freddy, and he never liked him anyway, so it's all the same. Now are you okay, Jessie?"

"Me? . . . Sure. I just don't want to get back in that freezing water again, if I can help it. How come it's so cold? It was almost warm at Westwater."

"I've been wondering about that too. I think it's because of the dam. We started off not far below Glen Canyon Dam, according to the map. In the ocean, the deeper you dive, the colder the water is. I bet they let the water out of the bottom of the lake."

We rejoined the group. Rita and Pug really wanted to

camp there on that beach. It was a tempting idea, and we started talking about collapsing right then and there. We were all exhausted, hadn't really slept since we left Colorado about thirty hours before. "Can we?" Rita pleaded with Troy. "Can we?"

Rita was sure Troy was going to say yes, but he didn't. "Judging from the road map, it looks like there's at least two hundred miles of river between Lee's Ferry and Lake Mead. Ten days of food . . . We'll have to cover over twenty miles a day."

"How do we estimate distance?" I asked.

"String," Adam volunteered.

"We can live off the land," Pug said gravely, as his hand went to his giant knife.

Adam looked around. "I dunno . . . The land don't look too edible in these parts."

Everybody agreed we'd better try to put on some miles.

Down the river we came to the biggest rapid yet. I thought, if they keep getting worse like this, I don't even want to think about how bad they could get. This one was on a turn, and the current was piling up against the cliff on the left in monstrous waves. Toward the bottom of the rapid, some of those waves poured over ledges into holes that looked as bad as that hole in Skull that Heather had come to know so intimately.

We scouted and talked strategy. The idea was to paddle out of that main current, to try to stay to the inside of the turn where there was a narrow strip of relatively calm water. The only problem was, all the current in the fast water would be pushing us toward the cliff and the big whitewater.

The longer you look at a rapid like that, the sicker you feel. Your insides churn, and your stomach does flips. The only relief is to get in the boats and just do it. When you secure the bowline and push off the bank, and you start drifting toward the lip of the rapid, it feels like you're about to jump out of an airplane or rob a bank or something. There's so much adrenalin in your system, you're giddy, sick, high, panicky, and courageous all at the same time.

But most of all, you're tuned in. You're right there. I heard Adam chant from behind me, "Let's head downriver, mates." I could see every little thing. I saw what the water was doing, I saw the bands of color on the cliff down on the left side where we didn't want to go, I saw a swallow skim the flat water on the top of the rapid, I saw Troy disappear over the edge, I noticed the woven friendship bracelet on Star's wrist. I heard the roar of the rapid and I heard a raven squawk. I felt the strength in my arms and my back and my legs. In answer to Adam's commands, I paddled with sweeping strokes to help move to the right. "Downriver!" I yelled.

As we approached the brink and could see the course of the rapid below us, I saw Troy's boat down toward the bottom. He was in the big stuff, exactly where he didn't want to be. Up against the cliffs, his boat slid over a ledge and dropped into a hole that stood his sixteen-foot boat straight up in the air. It looked certain to flip, but it dropped down rightside up and was spit out of the hole. It all happened in an instant, and then I lost sight.

We were in a major fight ourselves to get out of the current, and we were winning it. We paddled like anything for the inside of the turn, and we made it. We scooted past all the nasty water, barely out of its reach on that ribbon of safe water.

"We did it!" I shouted. "We're really doing it!"

Whatever the name of that rapid, our paddle crew celebrated a major victory. Adam was the man of the moment, and we all felt good about ourselves. We'd applied a strategy to a nasty-looking rapid, and it had worked. As we paddled up to him, Troy was methodically bailing out his boat. Somebody asked him how his run was, and he said, "Fine," but with little enthusiasm. I could tell from the reactions on the paddle raft that no one but I had seen him do that dramatic stand-up.

"Actually," Troy admitted, "this boat is pretty unstable with no weight up front—it wants to lift up on me. Jessie, would you come over and keep the front end down?"

There was a little snickering over that, but I suppose that was inevitable with Troy and me being friendly.

Under the circumstances, I wasn't sure I wanted to go over to the other boat, and I wasn't sure I wanted to give up paddling when I'd been enjoying it so much. There'd be nothing to do in the front of the rowed raft. Paddling up there would be pointless.

Adam could see my hesitation. "Go ahead, Jessie. You'd look great up there . . . kind of like those carved ladies they had on those old sailing ships."

"More like a hood ornament," Rita said.

"Okay, you guys," I said. "Stuff it." I stowed my paddle under the net holding the gear in the middle of the paddle raft, and I stepped over to Troy's boat, to the applause of my former shipmates. I wasn't going to let them sway me one way or the other. The bottom line was, I knew Troy needed me.

As we drifted downstream, I did feel a little like Troy's hood ornament, but I got over it. We liked each other, and I liked being with him on his boat. As the afternoon wore on, we had a sense that we were having our own separate experience. We talked a lot, mostly about the trip and, very softly, about the other people. Voices carry so easily on the river. We could hear everything they were saying on the other boat, even when they were way behind us.

The current picked up and we entered a wild stretch of river. There were rapids every half mile or so. Troy would stand up in the boat and look at the rapid coming up, and determine that scouting from the boat was sufficient without having to go to shore. I was glad. We were too tired to scramble around in the rocks and study every one of these rapids. "Read 'n' run!" he'd holler back to the paddle raft. "Read 'n' run!"

The next stretch was a wild time. I loved being in the front of the boat, taking all the big waves, and looking back to Troy at work on the oars. He really loved the whitewater. In the rapids he wore a wonderful grin all over his face, and his blue eyes were all concentration looking downstream. He was learning how to move that boat, how to spin it to avoid the rocks and holes. He was learning when to apply power and when to apply finesse.

I watched the runs the paddle raft was making behind us as well. I heard Adam saying that as long as he kept the boat straight, they could blow through the holes, and that's what they were doing, going intentionally for the action. He'd yell for them to power to the right or left, and then he'd rudder the boat directly for the hole. They were having a blast. I felt like I was missing something, but that was okay. I was doing just fine relaxing in the warm sunshine, and I loved having the time with Troy.

We could hear another rapid coming, but we couldn't see it because it was on a sharp turn. "Should we scout it?" I asked Troy. He wagged his head. He was taken with the string of successes behind us, and having too much fun rowing to want to pull the boat to shore, tie it up, and go for a look. We rounded the bend in the center of the river and caught sight of a major hole only thirty or so feet in front of us.

There was no time to cock the boat and row to either side. All Troy could do was hit the hole straight on. I speared my weight to the very front as we dropped into the hole, and then I felt the oddest sensation. We had stopped moving. We were surfing in place. Suddenly the hole spun us sideways, and one side of the boat lifted up in the air as the low side was filling with water. My eyes met Troy's for a minute. He was at a loss. I lunged for the high side, to try to put some weight on it. Just as suddenly, the hole spit us out. "Bail!" Troy yelled. We were suddenly knee-deep in water.

Around the bend came the paddle raft, only they were on the inside of the turn as they approached the hole. They would have missed it, but they were paddling like crazy to line up for it on purpose. When they dropped into it, the hole spun them sideways too. They had no more control than a stick of driftwood. The black underside of their boat showed for a moment, and then the boat turned over. They'd flipped!

I saw swimmers. A couple of people were bobbing along in the river; Adam was hanging onto the chicken line on the overturned boat. Troy bent his back to the oars and rowed toward an eddy, so we wouldn't be swept downstream. "Bail!" he yelled. "Boat's too heavy to row! Bail!"

I bailed like mad with that big bucket, and Troy caught the eddy. As the swimmers approached us, he rowed out into the current and I hauled Rita aboard. Troy intercepted Adam, who was clinging to the paddle raft. "We hit the hole straight on," Adam protested. "I don't know what happened."

Freddy and Pug, I could see, had reached the shore on their own, but where was Star?

"Over there!" I yelled, and pointed at Star in the river.

We dragged Star in. She was so weak, she couldn't help herself at all. She wasn't built with any insulation against that icy water, and as it turned out, she'd been held in the hole and given a thrashing.

We made a quick landfall, as Freddy and Pug ran downstream to join us. There was no beach there. It wasn't really a camp, but we had work to do, with the paddle raft to overturn, and little time—the sun was down from the canyon. We were all shivering, especially Star, whose eyes weren't even focusing. We had to get to the dry bags under the paddle raft, and put on some dry clothes. It took all of us, minus Star, to turn the boat over. Any kind of beach would've been handy, but there was a deep drop-off right at the bank. We had to use a lot of ropes, and pull on them with all our strength. For a while it looked like we wouldn't succeed. Three times the boat came about halfway up and then stalled. Adam said to Troy, "I sure hope that gear boat of yours never flips. It weighs about three times as much as this one."

We gave it one more try, and this time Pug went berserk, giving a ferocious battle cry and pulling on his rope like a Goliath. His mighty legs dug for traction, and in the end he fell into a pile of sharp rocks as the boat fell rightside up against the bank.

Pug came up full of scrapes and scratches, but he thought nothing of them, being the man of the moment and the recipient of truckloads of praise. He was beaming. That Dutch marine crewcut of his, about a month grown out, made him seem like a little fuzzball kid in a giant body, a little kid who only wanted the rest of the gang to like him. Rita went over to him and raised his right arm like a boxer's in triumph, then felt his biceps. "Hot stuff," she declared.

It was our first night in camp on the river. Nobody wanted to follow Al's work list, which was taped to the inside of the lid of the kitchen box. "Who needs it?" Troy said. We didn't set up the latrine, either. We were just too exhausted. "Just dig a cat hole behind a bush," Troy said.

Thank goodness Rita had some energy. She whipped dinner together—beef stroganoff, no less—and it was much appreciated. We did the dishes by lantern light, then crashed. None of us put up a tent. Exhausted doesn't begin to describe how I felt. Star and I spread our tent out and used it for a ground cloth. Star was pretty out of it, still in shock from her swim. "Are you okay?" I asked her, as I was falling asleep.

"Perfect," she said.

· 8 ·

AS IF I WEREN'T TIRED ENOUGH, MY DREAMS wouldn't let me get off the river, and I was paddling on and on in my sleep, tossing and turning, paddling for my life through ever-taller waves and gaping holes. Every moment was an emergency; the whitewater never let up. Finally we tipped up on a huge rock, and I was thrown overboard. Then I was tumbling and tossing among the surging waves, and I felt myself being swept away, farther and farther downriver, swept away, swept away. . . .

My own voice woke me up. Star's hand was on my shoulder. "You were having a nightmare," she said.

"It was awful. What was I saying?"

"You were calling for your mother."

"Are you sure?" I asked. I had no memory of dreaming about my mother. I was trembling, having a hard time even getting a fix on where I was. Then it all came back. The Grand Canyon . . .

"There's no way I'm going to be able to get back to sleep," I said.

"Me neither. I've been lying awake for hours."

"You want to take a walk down the shore? I can't just lie here, I'll go crazy."

We put on our jackets, which we were using for pillows, grabbed our flashlights and wool caps, and slipped out of camp. Even in the desert, it was cold at night, at least in October. We found a little sandy beach a way downstream, sat down huddled side by side, and turned off our flashlights. For a long while we didn't speak, but watched the sliver of a moon set, and then took in the light of a billion stars playing on the surface of the river. Close by, the water was reverberating on a willow shoot, and from upstream came the dull roar of the rapid that Star and the others had swum. The seconds slowed, and then the minutes slowed, and I could feel a fear creeping into my bones and taking me over, a sort of fear I'd only had glimpses of before. Maybe it was the sort that prehistoric people felt, knowing how small and defenseless they were against the huge nothingness of it all. I felt like I was being crushed by the immensity of the darkness, the river, the walls, the stars. My heart was pounding, I felt like crying out. It came to me for the first time, the full realization of what I had done.

A shooting star made a long and instantaneous track from above us downriver. "Did you see that?" asked Star.

"Yes," I answered. "Wasn't it sad? Our lives are like that, don't you think?"

"Oh no . . . it's a good sign."

"I remember. Silver starlight—your soul color."

For a while we didn't speak again, and then I said, "In

my nightmare, I was drowning, but you're the one who was really out in the river, and you had a bad swim, like Heather's."

"I did," she said tentatively.

"How do you do it?"

"Do what?"

"Stay so calm."

"I try to think positive."

"Like when we lay down to sleep, and I asked how you were, and you said, 'perfect.'"

She didn't reply.

"Did you feel perfect?" I asked gently.

Her hand went to the crystal around her neck. "I was so scared, Jessie, but I can't think about it. I have to keep preparing the path I'm going to walk on."

"You don't think it was your fault that you got thrown out of the boat, do you?"

"I have to try harder, keep my concentration."

"You 'imaged' it?"

"Maybe I did. . . ."

"If you image something in your dreams, does that make it happen?"

"I don't know," she said. She knew what I was thinking—was I going to drown on this trip?

"Do you ever have bad dreams . . . nightmares?" I asked her.

"I do," she answered slowly. "Mostly about my mother. She left me when I was about seven."

When Star didn't continue, I said, "My mother died from cancer when I was five. She went away to the hospital, and my dad took me to see her a few times . . . he told me she was going to die, but I don't think I understood what that meant. Then one day he told me she was dead. I never saw her again. At the funeral her casket was closed. I thought for the longest time she would be coming back. I would dream she was back. . . ."

"I know," Star said softly, with more emotion in her voice than I'd ever heard before. "It was like that for me too. We were always moving around, never staying long in one place. Then one time she took me to this shelter—some kind of a church home, with a lot of other families, living like in a dormitory. We were only there a few days when she said she was going out and she'd be right back. She never came back."

I was starting to speak, about to suggest that maybe her mother was abducted or murdered. But Star shook her head. "She didn't want me. I waited for months, I waited for years, in institutions, foster homes. People would tell me things happened to her, but deep down I knew. She just didn't want me."

I hugged her close. "I'm so sorry, Star."

As I hugged her I realized why she didn't mix with everybody. It wasn't because she was shy. She wasn't really a teenager, like the rest of us. She wasn't a child or an adult either. Star was her own creation, and not by choice. It must be so lonely, I thought, being her.

"It's my karma," Star said. "I can't feel sorry for myself. Jessie, you know the part I think about the most? When my mother left, she was pregnant. That means I have a sister or a brother out there somewhere. I feel like it's a sister, and I think about her a lot. Maybe someday our paths will cross, and we'll know. . . ."

"What about your father?" I asked softly.

"I don't have any idea who he was."

"How long did you live out on the street?"

"Basically, the last two years."

"What city?"

"Portland, and then Los Angeles."

"You don't need to tell me this, but . . . is it as awful as they say . . . the things you have to do to survive?"

"It is, Jessie. It really is."

"There's so much cruelty in the world," I said. I couldn't find the words. I couldn't really know or appreciate what she'd been through, I realized, but I could sure understand her crystals and her Tarot deck a whole lot better. It was her only protection.

"You're so lucky to have a father, Jessie. He's not cruel, is he?"

"Oh no, he doesn't have a mean bone in his body. But we're definitely not getting along right now. I feel terrible about it."

"It'll get better, Jessie."

"You really think so?"

She gave me a hug. "Dawn's coming," she said, pointing to the faint light over the rim of the canyon. "A brand new day."

Just then came the song of the canyon wren, that rich, clean cascade of slowing and falling whistles, as the canyon walls began to catch the faint glow of dawn. We looked at each other and smiled.

"Whatever happens," I told her, "We have each other. Friends, come what may—agreed?"

Star smiled, and her smile didn't seem quite so forlorn.

I tugged at the woven friendship bracelet around her ankle. "Anyway I think your theory about imaging is a bunch of bull. If it were true, I'd be rich from imaging myself winning the lottery."

She laughed, and then she untied the bracelet from her ankle. For a moment she held it against the one on her wrist, and then she said, "Would you keep it, to remember me by?"

"Tie it on my wrist for me. But what's this, 'to remember me by' stuff?"

"Nothing," she said. "You know. . . ."

We started back to camp. "What a night," I said.

Ahead we could see a little fire going. It made a cheerful sight.

⋄ 9 ⋄

FREDDY WAS SITTING BY THE CAMPFIRE AND cradling a steaming cup of coffee in his hands. "Care for some?" he asked, and then fetched cups for us out of the kitchen box. "Got a few grounds," he cautioned. The three of us sat around for almost an hour drinking coffee and watching the glow on the canyon walls turn a richer and richer gold while waiting for the others to get up. We didn't talk much, but Freddy was easy to be around. He and Star were talking about birds, and it was interesting. Freddy was saying he mostly knew about birds in the mountains. I was looking across the river, and I noticed that the water level had dropped drastically overnight. The river had an ugly bathtub ring of mud and rocks maybe twelve feet high. "The river sure has gone down," I remarked.

"A lot," Freddy agreed. "You want to see something?"

"Sure," I said.

"It isn't very pretty."

He led us over to where the boats were tied. They were a startling sight, hanging almost vertically from their ropes. It looked as if someone had pulled the plug on the river. "I tried to lower them," Freddy said, "but they're hung up on those rocks. I hope nothing fell out."

After everybody else was up, we clustered on the top of the bank and talked about our predicament. It turned out we lost the spare paddle and the spare life jacket. They weren't tied down and they'd simply fallen off the back of the gear boat. We agreed we weren't going to leave the boats on a drop-off again, and we heaped abuse on the engineers at the dam who jerk the river up and down, depending, we concluded, on how much electricity they want to generate at any given time. We talked about what we were going to do about it: wait for the river to rise or work like slaves to free the boats. We went to work. The water level, we noticed as we were standing there talking, was still going down.

At last we were floating in the sunshine once again. Troy had his shirt off and I was sitting on the gear lashed behind him, chattering away and massaging his shoulders with lotion. "It could have been worse," I was saying.

"I just hope they hang on to their paddles."

"We still have mine, which makes an extra."

I jumped to the front as we approached a rapid. We ran it and then a second with no problem at all. The paddle raft was sticking close, and they were doing fine too. Adam had given the rudder position and the captainship over to Freddy, who was a natural.

Ahead on the right side an amazing sight came into view: bright green hanging gardens and two waterfalls bursting out of caves in the cliff. Troy and I were first to see them, and we shared the moment. "I can't believe this," I said. "What a paradise!"

Troy nodded proudly and rowed for the shore.

We parked at the foot of the oasis where the cave-fed creek met the river, and we all hiked up to the foot of the falls. Most of us hiked up and around, but Pug, who was eager to join us, came charging right up through the greenery like a rogue elephant. Freddy hollered down that he thought that stuff might be poison ivy. Freddy's warning slowed Pug's rampage for about two seconds, and then he came on through.

Adam, who was as nimble as those Ninja warriors he so admired, soon scrambled up the step-like terraces high into the waterfall and actually gained the mouth of the caves. Freddy quickly joined him. It was quite a sight to see those two standing up there. Adam actually squeezed into one of the caves alongside the jet of water. One slip, I'm sure, and he would have been jetted onto the slippery stairs and all the way down to where we were standing.

Star and I climbed halfway up to the cave, where the falls fanned out onto the stairs, and we sat on moss-covered benches in the rippling water. Alongside us a world of ferns and wildflowers took in the spray. It seemed like a glorious way to live. I said to Star, "If I were to be reincarnated as a plant, I wouldn't mind living right here. And look at the view!"

At the foot of the falls was a small pool, and four of us took turns sitting in it and letting the little creek pound on our shoulders while we waited for Freddy and Adam to come down. Pug was off to the side, sitting atop a boulder, looking worried and starting to scratch.

Back on the river, we floated below the mouth of a large cave perched at about the same level as those that spouted the falls, and Adam had us all quickly paddling for shore. He was sure we could get up there, and he was sure the cave mouth was a mere doorstep to a fabulous network of caverns.

Out came the ropes. The idea was, everybody was supposed to get up to the cave and explore it. Adam was certain we could all do it. He kept pointing out the route. "There's only one rough spot. Freddy or I can go up with the rope."

I was thrilled, of course, remembering my most recent climbing adventure. Adam came over and lobbied me pretty hard. I started out with the rest. Only Star stayed behind. I went along, not because of Adam's persuasion, but because I knew I had a hang-up to get over. Maybe even more than that, because I didn't want to miss anything.

We got up there all right, every one of us. With Adam and Freddy up above, and Troy giving me an assist from below, I made it up the rope, and this time I remembered Freddy's advice on Storm King: "Jessie, don't look down."

It was quite a feeling, and an accomplishment, to stand in the mouth of that cave. I felt pretty good about myself. I waved to Star down by the boats, and she waved back. As we stood there another group floated by—three boats. They saw us up there, and they hollered their appreciation. People in their twenties and thirties, it looked like. They sure weren't nosy or suspicious about us. Maybe from that distance they couldn't tell how young we were. Soon their boats were tiny in the distance and drifting around the bend. "Perfect timing," Troy said. "We didn't have to visit with them."

Everybody started talking about Heather, wondering if she'd squealed on us. "Maybe not," Troy said. "Looks like we're in the clear."

Pug was scratching away at the rising rash on his arms, neck, and face. "Don't scratch it," Troy told him. "You'll make it worse."

We turned to explore the cave. It wasn't Carlsbad Caverns, but then we never got to the end of it, either. We came to a big room full of fountains of stone, and we stopped there and poked around. On a wall, my flashlight illuminated patterns—handprints. "Over here," I said. There were dozens of them, a deep red, some apparently made by pressing a hand dipped in pigment against the wall, and some made by pigment blown everywhere but where the hand was. I knew how they were made; my dad had explained it to me.

"Cavemen," Rita said. "Incredible!"

"Check out the gazelles," Troy said, discovering a parade of horned animals farther down the wall.

Bighorn sheep, I realized. I saw Freddy smiling. He and I were both from this part of the country. Rock art like this was quite common, the work of Anasazi cliff dwellers from about a thousand years ago. He gave me a little wink, and neither of us corrected Troy about his gazelles.

On the way down from the mouth of the cave, Adam, in his casual manner, got a little careless and kicked a rock loose, a small but hardly harmless rock. It caught Rita, who was just below him, right on the scalp line and opened up a gusher of a head wound. In an instant the fun was over. This was going to be serious.

I'd barely come down, and was standing with Troy at the base of the drop when Rita was hit. She was still on the rope. The rock could just as easily have sailed by her and struck me or Troy. Rita clung to the rope as blood ran down her face and onto her T-shirt. She cursed up at Adam and he said lamely, "Sorry." She cursed him again, and then dropped beside me. I grabbed her legs as she was falling and hung on to her. Her blood was getting all over me too. It was frightening how much blood there was. Rita was so scared, she didn't know what to do, and I sat her down fast and pressed the palm of my hand hard against the wound to stop the bleeding. "I need something—I need a compress," I told Troy, and he mumbled, "I can't stand the sight of blood."

Adam, who was watching from above, whipped off his T-shirt, tore out a patch of material, and tossed it down to me. Troy was already on his way down to the boats. I couldn't believe he was just going to walk off like that, but that's what he did. I walked Rita slowly down to the boats, holding the compress tightly against her head. Her blood was all caked in her thick black hair, and she looked a mess. Her olive complexion had gone white. "We need to do something," I said to Freddy, who was springing off the gear boat with the rocket box marked FIRST AID. None of us had even looked in it before. "Lemme see how bad," he said, and I lifted the compress so he could see. The wound started bleeding again, but not as badly as before.

I said, "I don't know what kind of bandage would work."

"Needs stitches," Freddy said.

"Stitches!" Rita yelled. "You gotta be kidding!"

She started to swoon. I had her sit down. "Freddy," I said, "on the inside of the lid—see if it says anything about stitches on the list."

Freddy was looking at the paper, but he wasn't even focusing. Was he going to be useless too? "What's the matter?" I said impatiently. "Does it have stitches or not?"

"I can't read very good," he said quietly. He looked away. I'd made him feel ashamed. I had no idea. . . .

"I'm sorry," I said, and asked him to hold the compress while I read Al's typewritten and laminated list on the inside of the lid. "Suture kit," I called out, and started hunting for it. "Now where does that get us? I've never done stitches."

Everybody was crowding around by this time, except for Troy, who was hanging back. He looked as pale as Rita. I guess it was true what he said about how he couldn't take the sight of blood. Me, on the other hand, I'd make a pretty good emergency nurse, if I knew anything, that is.

"I can do it," Freddy said.

Nobody was going to take the job away from him.

"Are you sure?" Rita said. "Don't I get a shot or anything?"

"Good question," I said, and looked through the list hoping to find some kind of local anesthetic. No such luck. Apparently Al wasn't a practicioner of painless surgery.

The cut was right on Rita's hairline. Freddy called for a razor, soap and water, and peroxide. Adam had recovered enough to hang around and banter with Rita, who was starting to enjoy being the center of attention, now that she could see she wasn't going to drop dead.

When Freddy was set, Adam yelled "Hold everything," then scurried along the water line and came running back with a small driftwood stick. "For her to bite on," he explained. "Like in the movies."

Up close, I watched Freddy sew as Rita stifled the screams. She bit down hard on that stick, tears running down her face. Pug was holding her head still, and was clearly enjoying the job.

Freddy's fingers were quick and deft. It was obvious he knew what he was doing. He made one stitch, toward one end of the cut, and then tied it with a twist of the needle pliers. Then he did a stitch at the other end. "I would've thought you sewed like you do with clothes," I remarked. "You know, around and around with the same thread. How come you know how to do this?"

He smiled. "Oh, I've sewed up plenty of sheep."

At that the driftwood stick went flying from Rita's mouth, and everybody was laughing. "Sheep! He's sewed up sheep! I am not a sheep!"

One more stitch in the middle, and Freddy was done. Rita fought her way free of Pug's embrace and ran after Adam, who was blatting at her in an uncannily sheeplike manner. "Come back here, you Ninja assassin scumbag!"

It was midafternoon already. We ate lunch, and there was talk about camping as soon as possible. Nobody really wanted to press on, even if we hadn't covered our miles for the day; we'd make them up tomorrow. Before long we came to an immense overhang on river left. We beached and ran up under that roof. The cavern was like a domed stadium, with a playing surface of fine sand. The ever-playful Adam sprinted back to the boats and returned with a pie plate to toss around. We quickly agreed that we'd never find a better camp.

We threw the pie tin around until we were exhausted from all the running. Even Star joined in for a little bit, though she couldn't really throw or catch very well. It was good to see she was feeling better, and focusing again.

After a while Star and Rita and I drifted way down to the end of the cavern along the water line. We had a project—getting Rita cleaned up and back to normal. Now that the emergency had passed she was pretty distressed about her appearance. With all the dried blood on her face and in her hair, she did look like a massacre victim.

It took quite a bit of my bottle of shampoo and a lot of careful work around the stitched cut to restore her hair to normal. She had such thick, black hair, and it was all matted together, almost glued. My fingers worked the suds in while Star poured water gently from a bail bucket. We even gave Rita the creme rinse treatment after the shampoo. Rita really settled down. I wouldn't have thought, as perpetually hyperactive as she was, that she had it in her to sit still like this. The way the three of us were, it was almost as if we were performing a ritual, and Rita felt very soothed by it all.

Now if we could just keep her hair from getting into the stitches while the cut was healing. "A French braid," I thought aloud. "Rita, how would you like your hair in a French braid? I can do it, and I think it would look really nice."

For once, Rita didn't seem to know what to say. I'll bet she never had anyone fussing over her hair before. I didn't wait for an answer, just started parting her thick hair into sections and braiding it. Not too tight, I told myself, so it doesn't pull on the cut and the stitches. We were sitting a few feet back from the water, in the warmth of the sunshine, and feeling good. Star left for a few minutes and then returned with her Tarot deck. As I was braiding Rita's hair, the wildwoman closed her eyes, faced the sun, and discovered the power of meditation for what I would guess was the first time in her life. Star spread out her blue silk scarf a little way down the beach, scribbled a question on her notepad, and slowly began to lay out the cards.

None of the three of us spoke. Rhythmically braiding Rita's hair, I'd glance from Star to the river, to the cliffs, and back to Star. The song of the canyon wren was there with us, water and music blended together and piped from the throat of that nondescript little bird. Such an ordinary-looking bird, I thought, to give voice to the essence of the canyon. The reflections, the subtle lapping of the calm water against the margins of the river, the crystalline quality of the light in the pure, dry air—all of it was expressed in that falling stream of droplets that was the canyon wren's song. Whatever happens downstream, I thought, this beauty right here, right now, makes it all worthwhile.

The moment took me back to times with my dad. There'd been times like this one, more than a few. One I'll never forget was when we watched a sunset from the top of one of Colorado's fourteen-thousand-foot peaks, Mount Wilson, and we saw those hundreds and hundreds of peaks in the Uncompahgre and the San Juans all bathed in that glowing light. I found myself wishing my dad could be on the river with me, that it could be like it was in the years before it all got so confusing. He would appreciate it so much. Gone are the days, I thought. I wonder if I'll ever share those feelings with my dad again, now that he has Madeline.

I'd finished braiding Rita's hair. My hands were still. She really looked pretty with her hair pulled back like that. Neither of us spoke for a while, and then she said "Thanks, Jessie," and got up and wandered back to the kitchen, where almost miraculously the guys were cooking dinner all by themselves. I went over and sat by Star, and looked at all the pretty cards laid out in front of her. The sunlight had left the beach and goose bumps were popping up on my arms. Star turned to me with a look of relief. "What is it, Star?" I asked. "What's the Outcome?"

With a delighted look on her face, she held up a card that said, "the Star." It depicted a young girl pouring water from two vases, one into a clear pool, and one onto the shore. In the background was a ring of stars encircling one large star. "Pretty special," I said. "What does the Star mean?"

"Inspiration and hope—spiritual gifts."

"Good," I said. "I'm so pleased for you." I was happy to have Star feeling better, even if it took the cards. Good thing she hadn't thrown some awful, scary reading.

The guys were beating the propane bottle with the crescent wrench, our dinner bell as it were, and Pug was hollering at us for good measure in the voice of a little boy who's discovered himself doing something good and was anxious to have admiration heaped upon him. I'd be happy to oblige. I was hungry.

As I was getting up I noticed a bright star rising on the horizon, encircled with companions. "Look, Star! Especially for you."

That night everybody sat around a bonfire of driftwood, enjoying the glowing warmth of the flames. We talked and we laughed, we heard a few stories. Adam was a master storyteller, mostly of autobiographical tales. I wasn't doing much talking. I was with Troy, leaning back against him and enjoying the feel of his arms around me. Troy and I stayed, talking softly, long after everyone else drifted away. I asked him what it was like going to private schools back East. He told me he'd been kicked out of the last three, for not following the rules and showing other kids they didn't have to, either. "I'm so tired of all that," he said. "I want to get on with my life." At his last school, the one where he was before he came to Hoods in the Woods, he lasted only two weeks. I got the feeling something more serious had happened there, but he didn't elaborate, so I let it drop. Our whispering meandered into the night along happier paths, until finally we weren't speaking at all. There was just the sound of the river, that incredible starry sky, and us. The King of Hearts . . . the cards were right.

· 10 ·

WE FLOATED ON, PUTTING THE MILES BEHIND us and quickly losing track of the days. I found myself thinking less and less of everything I'd left behind. Maybe it's because you're literally moving downstream, with no chance of going back. You realize, as the cliffs slide by, that the past really is gone forever.

Clear blue skies, good company—this was the life. I was even learning how to row the boat. Troy wasn't inclined to teach me, but he didn't mind letting me get in some time on the oars. He'd stretch out and take catnaps while I experimented with turning the boat around, avoiding obstacles, and getting the boat to shore for landings. It was pretty different from the paddle raft.

We floated by side-canyon after side-canyon. I could tell that Freddy, over on the other boat, was distressed. He would look longingly at the openings of those canyons, gleaming with polished rock and often running with clear water. He hated to see them slipping by. They looked so inviting, I wished I could explore them myself. From the rudder, Freddy looked back at them again and again between strokes, as if memorizing them for future reference.

In camp we had our routines down pretty well. Much of the shore time was taken up with de-rigging the boats, hauling all the gear up the beach, setting up the kitchen, cooking, doing dishes, hauling the gear down the beach, and rigging the boats.

There was always a little time, though, for goofing around or washing your clothes or doing whatever you wanted to do. Actually there was more free time for some than for others. Adam was usually off trying in vain to catch what he called the "Indy 500 Lizards," while Pug was attending to his poison ivy in his own way, scraping the blisters open with the sharp edge of his buck knife. Troy would hang around the kitchen and provide charm. His freedom was part of his mystique as trip leader and captain of the gear boat.

One morning we came to the biggest side-canyon of them all, and there was no question about floating by this one. The stream issuing from it was robin's egg blue, a remarkable sight. No one had ever seen anything like it, except Troy, who mentioned to me that it reminded him of the ocean water in the Caribbean. We tied up our boats and wandered upstream along what we quickly named the River of Blue.

Before long we discovered that the water was actually warm, in contrast to the freezing water of the Colorado, and we all went swimming. In between dips we sunbathed against the ready-made backrests at the foot of the cliffs.

Somebody remembered that we'd left two feet of snow behind in Colorado, and it didn't even seem possible, it was so warm here.

Pug said, "We really miss Al bad. Troy, don't you miss Al?"

"Al who?"

"Yeah, right . . ."

Adam came walking by, in his bare feet as usual, and slowly made tracks across the cracked mudflat just upstream from us. The clay oozed up between his toes—a most delightful consistency. Before long he succumbed to gravity and sat there in the mud, reaching for gobs of it, which he proceeded to rub all over his body, even his face. Rita helped him out with his back, carefully applying the mud all around his eyes, and then heaped a cone of mud on top of his head. He had us in hysterics, as usual. Before long, all seven of us were sitting in a circle, encased in mud. "We're the Mudheads," I said. "The Mudheads Do the Grand Canyon."

Pug was maybe the most delighted of all. "I can't feel my poison ivy! It doesn't itch a bit!"

It wasn't long before Adam discovered, a little upstream, a section of the stream bank that was all clay. He sprinted back to the boats, returned with a bail bucket, and began madly splashing the incline with water. Then he ran up to the top of the bank and slid down it like a human otter, splashing into the blue stream. Everyone else joined in. "It doesn't get any better than this!" Pug bellowed. "Say, Troy, no more miles today, okay? Let's stay here."

"We did a lot of miles the last few days," Troy said. "Fine with me."

DOWNRIVER

Within a few minutes, Freddy was heading upstream. He waded across the River of Blue, and then started up the other side. I realized he was going to explore this side-canyon, and I knew immediately that I wanted to go with him. "Hey, wait a minute, Freddy," I called out. I dived into the warm blue water and came up stroking. As I walked through the shallows on the other side, I could see that Freddy was waiting for me and was looking a little puzzled. Troy called out, "Where you going, Jessie?"

"Up the canyon with Freddy," I called back. "Wanna come?"

"How're you going to beat this?"

"I just want to see what there is to see."

He'd made himself pretty comfortable in the sun. "You go ahead," he said. "Have a good time."

Freddy waited for me to catch up, but when I did, he wasn't overjoyed. "I want to see how far I can go," he said. "I'm going to go fast."

His dark eyes met mine for the briefest of moments, and then he looked away again. He wasn't at all sure of me.

"I'll keep up," I said. "I'd really like to go."

He shrugged, and we started up the River of Blue, relatively slowly at first, but ever quicker as Freddy saw I could keep up. Through boulder fields and across slickrock terraces, along bits of deer trails, across the stream again when we'd get cliffed out on one side: This was my kind of cross-country hiking. My dad and I used to do it all the time. A couple of times Freddy glanced back, and flashed a brief smile to see I was right with him. I could move almost as quietly as he. My father called it "the Zen of rock hopping." The art is that you never think about it—you

99

don't plan your route in a conscious way. Your whole body is reacting to the ever-changing pattern of the landscape, and you just go with your body. If you're into it just right, you can do outrageous feats, incredible jumps, pinpoint landings. Your timing is perfect. You're as at home on the rocks as a mountain goat.

A couple of miles up the canyon, I switched into another gear. Just for the fun of it, because I was feeling so good and Freddy's stated objective was to see how far he could go, I broke into a jog and blew by him. Now it was my turn to pick the route, and I loved it. This was advanced Zen. I had to scan ahead for the best route while staying totally tuned in to my next few steps. We went flying up the canyon, and neither of us was breathing that hard.

I kept running as I was passing a formation off on my left, but then I slowed when I realized what an odd and unlikely sight it was, even in these canyons where bizarre formations are commonplace: a dome of gold-brown mineral deposits, standing on its own in the flats beside the blue stream. Like a little volcano, I thought, only shaved off flat on the top.

As Freddy caught up with me, I became aware that I had almost stepped on something startlingly strange and beautiful, and I stooped to pick it up. A pair of sticks, whittled smooth and stained blue, topped with a large feather and wrapped with handspun white yarn, securing sprigs of herbs, downy feathers, and a pointed bit of corn husk. A loose end of yarn held another, smaller feather and some pine needles. I was holding something fashioned by human hands, but seemingly of another age.

"What in the world?" I wondered aloud. "Look, there's more of them."

I gave the one in my hands to Freddy, whose eyes went from it to the dome, now shining strikingly orange in the shifting light. Preoccupied and confused, he walked quietly over to the mysterious formation and climbed to the top.

I joined him up there, and found him sitting beside a small pool, a fountain bubbling golden water up from the earth. From the secret places, I thought. From another world.

The amber stream trickled off the far side of the dome, and as I looked that way, my eye picked up feathers in the bushes here and there on the flats below, and then I saw more and more of the stick-pairs. "They're all over," I said. "Freddy, they're all over."

I turned to Freddy, wanting him to stand up and see what I had discovered, when I found that tears were welling from his dark eyes. "What is it, Freddy?" I whispered. I sat down beside him and looked into the fountain, but I couldn't see the depths that he was seeing. "What is it?"

"This is a shrine," he said. "It's called the *sipapuni*. And this is a *paho*," he added, holding up the little bundle I'd almost stepped on. "A prayer stick."

"Shrine? Whose shrine?"

"The Hopis. The Hopi Indians." Freddy wiped his eyes, and shook his head. "I never thought about it coming down the river, never even remembered. I still wouldn't have realized what this place was unless you'd seen this, and put it in my hand. Right here's where the Hopis believe that the people came into this world—through the *sipapuni*. I grew up hearing about it—this is the one place my mother always wanted me and my father to see. He never got here to see it."

Freddy brushed more tears from his eyes. "And now, here I am."

"You're a Hopi?"

He sighed. "My mother is a Hopi. She's gone back to Second Mesa now, in Arizona, but I'm not really from there. I wasn't raised as a Hopi. My mother would tell me things, though. She told me about the *sipapuni* when I was little, and about some of the old stories and customs. There are lots of rituals . . . a lot with running great distances—she said I would like that part. Young men run across the desert to visit the *sipapuni* and leave *pahos.*"

"What about your father, Freddy?"

"My father . . . he's dead. He always said we should visit here one day. He felt sorry that his work took us away from my mother's people. He was a Basque—from Spain."

"What did he do? How did he get to America?"

"He was a sheepherder, the best." Freddy chuckled a little, and then said, "They can't get anybody to stay with the sheep over here, so the people who own the big flocks bring over Basques to do it."

Freddy looked at me for a second, wondering if he should go on, and then he did. "That high country above Al's camp in Colorado, that's right where we used to take our sheep. That's where we always lived in the summers."

"When we were at our base camp, you were always taking off by yourself. Was that where you were going?"

"Oh, there's a little lake up there, just above timberline. We'd move the sheep around, but that was always our favorite camp. We lived in a big sheepherder tent, me and my mother and father, and we always had horses and dogs. In the winters we went down into New Mexico with the sheep."

"You were really close to your father?"

Freddy nodded. In the quiet spell that followed he looked so sad and so alone. Finally he looked at me almost hopefully, and said, "Four years ago, he was killed by the police. It was all a big misunderstanding. He thought they were coming to take me away—there'd been talk about taking me to a boarding school. He picked up his rifle when they came. The police thought he was going to shoot. . . ."

"I'm sorry," I said. "I'm really sorry."

A raven came in with thrashing wings and landed nearby.

Freddy glanced at me as if recognizing for the first time who he was talking to, and he got up. He seemed embarrassed that he'd told me all this. He said, "We better get back."

"Freddy," I couldn't help asking, "how come you don't live with your mother?"

He hesitated, then began to speak again. "I tried . . . we went back to Second Mesa and lived with her family. But you can't *become* a Hopi, you have to be born one, raised one. I got into a lot of trouble."

We left the *sipapuni,* and started back down the canyon. The sun was high up on the walls, and it was getting late. Even so, we didn't run or even hustle. We walked very deliberately, Freddy in front and me behind. We didn't talk. I'd felt close to him there at the shrine, but with every step back toward the others I felt the distance growing, until it was almost as great as before. My thoughts were jumbled with conflicting emotions. I was thinking about Freddy going back to that lake to remember his dad. I was thinking about me and my dad, even about me and Freddy.

Back at camp everything felt different. It wasn't just that the others weren't still cavorting like otters; the whole mood had swung to the downside since we'd left them. I picked it up first off Rita and Pug—the cold wave was easy to notice. "What's the matter?" I asked Rita. "Did something happen here?"

"Nothing happened here," she said sarcastically. "We've been sitting around for hours, that's all. We could've been back on the river, and found a decent camp. Now we'll have to camp here, on these ledges."

"Wait a minute," I said. "Don't I remember Pug saying, 'No more miles,' and Troy saying we'd camp here?"

"We changed our minds," Pug explained. "We wanted to get back on the river. But you weren't around. Finally we had to give up and stay here."

I looked for Troy. He was lying back in the boatman's seat on the gear boat. "I'm sorry we got our signals crossed," I told him. "I thought we were camping here."

"No big deal," he said unconvincingly. His blue eyes weren't so warm. "I never thought you two would be gone long, that's all. My mistake . . ."

He seemed so disappointed in me. I could see now, it probably hadn't taken that long before they'd played themselves out on the otter slide. "I'm sorry, Troy. I didn't mean to create problems."

"Just think of the group, Jessie. That's what I try to do."

I returned to my tent, and was happy to find Star inside. I asked her if she knew why the winds had changed.

"It's Troy," she said. "He's the Magician, a man of influence, for good or ill. I asked the cards."

" 'Magician' . . . 'man of influence' . . . you asked a question about Troy, and that's really what it said? How come you were asking about him?"

"I've been thinking about him."

"He's not in a very good mood," I said. "I wonder what the real problem is."

"You and Freddy, maybe?"

"Just taking a hike?"

"Oh, I think it's great. I really like Freddy."

"I hate this. Things get so complicated. Let's make dinner—maybe that will perk everybody up."

As we were quietly preparing dinner, Adam came in with a plastic soap case and ceremoniously opened it up on the kitchen table for our inspection. Out crawled a yellowish scorpion, about two inches long and ready to do battle, with its stinger held high. Adam teased it with a straw. "Check out the claws! He's like a little lobster!"

Everyone else came around to see what the stir was about, and watched Adam's finger-length straw fence with the scorpion among the onions I was dicing at the time. The chancy part was, the scorpion's direction of travel was totally unpredictable. "Watch this," Rita said. "Our Ninja is about to get stung."

It was interesting, watching everybody's reactions. It was good theater for everyone but Star. "Don't say that," she told Rita. "It'll make it happen."

"Adam, lemme kill it for you," Pug offered. "Let's roast him in the flame."

"Hey, no way, big guy. I'm keepin' him alive."

Adam proceeded to recapture the scorpion in his blue soap case. He snapped the lid shut and tucked the case into the back pocket of his jeans. "Old Japanese saying," Adam said. "Live scorpion in pants make life interesting."

Troy said, "Don't sit down, old buddy."

In the morning I was back on Troy's boat, and it was easy to see we weren't the same as before. I tried to work on it, with forced cheerfulness, but he was in a foul mood. It wasn't hard to figure out that he was teaching me a lesson. The current picked up, and Troy worked the oars in lively water. He could pretend I wasn't there. Over on the other boat, they were enjoying themselves, and I was feeling like the captain's captive.

We left the confines of the narrow canyon we'd been in since we started, and entered a new realm. Finally it looked like the Grand Canyon I'd seen in pictures. Suddenly we could see miles and miles ahead and all the way up through layers and layers of formations to what had to be the very rim in the distance. I wished I felt happier about it. But I was all preoccupied. Should I wait him out, try to reason with him, beg his forgiveness, or tell him off and get on the other boat?

I heard my dad saying how I tend to see everything in extremes. "Everything is either wonderful or it's 'blown.'" Slow down, I told myself. Give it some time. Maybe Troy's just having a bad day. After all, we have been together constantly for quite a while now. This is bound to happen.

DOWNRIVER

Before long we noticed a little knob on the rim, with a distinctly unnatural look to it. For miles we floated in that direction. In between rapids we kept looking up to that rim, as the knob gradually assumed the lines of a tall stone tower.

"Hey," Pug yelled, filled with sudden inspiration. "There's probably tourists up in that tower checking us out with telescopes. Let's moon 'em!" When nobody signed up, Pug declined to take on the job by himself. "No guts, no glory," he grumbled.

In the late afternoon, we lost sight of the tower. We figured we must be pretty close to it and about five thousand feet below. After a roller coaster ride that lasted for miles, the current almost died out, and Troy had to turn his back downstream and pull on the oars through the nearly dead water. We turned a corner, and the River Thunder turned up the loudest yet. "This has to be a big one," Troy shouted back to the others. "We better scout it."

We made for a beach on the left just short of the brink of the rapid. The Thunder overwhelmed me and made me feel sick in the pit of my stomach and light-headed at the same time. Star and I were tying the bowlines to the bushy trees, and we could see we were both scared. We knew this one would be the worst yet. "What is it, a waterfall?" Star joked weakly.

We joined the others for the scout as we all stumbled down the left side for a look. The rapid was strewn with boulders from one side of the river to the other. The white water continued as far as we could see, through a maze of rocks and holes. A real mess. It was a dramatic spot, with the roar of the rapid and a new formation of stone walls breaking out of the riverbed at a steep angle and heading skyward into a dark gorge. I felt sicker than ever. Finding a route down through the first drop was going to be hard enough, and then we'd have to make a series of moves more difficult than any we'd done yet, to make it through the obstacle course below.

Freddy and Troy were on the highest boulder, tracing a possible route, when Rita yelled and pointed to a guy with a pack on his back coming toward us. He was leaping from boulder to boulder, really moving.

It was Al, in his marine fatigues. Dressed for battle, I thought.

Nobody said a thing.

Al scrambled over, jumped to a boulder right by us, and gave us a big smile, a classic mix of amusement and anger. Al, our ex-leader, in the flesh.

"May I offer my services?" he said.

$\diamond$ **11** $\diamond$

AL'S EYES WENT FROM PUG'S BUCK KNIFE IN its sheath to Pug's face. "Good case of poison ivy you've got there, Pug. I see you discovered the falls at Vasey's Paradise."

Pug only grunted. Then Al looked into our eyes, one person at a time. It was obvious he wasn't afraid of Pug or any of us. It was more as if he was asking how we could do this to him. He shook his head. "So what do you guys think you're doing?" he said.

"What are we doing?" Adam repeated melodramatically. "What are we doing? We are . . . *searching,* that's it, we are all searching for something. Some are searching for justice, others for lost honor, others for gold, glory, or enlightenment. Some of us are searching for the Northwest Passage, some the Lost Continent of Mu, others a mislaid toothbrush. Some of us are searching for the cure to cancer, others seek to mend broken hearts—"

"How 'bout the San Juan River?" Al suggested wryly. "Are any of you searching for that?"

"We were afraid of it," Troy said sarcastically. "We thought you were going to kill us all. We thought we should tune up first."

"Yeah," Pug added. "Get in some practice."

Al pointed to the big water. "Hance Rapid should be a good tune-up. At this water level, it's about a nine on a ten-scale."

"Done fine so far," Rita blurted out.

"Look," Al said decisively, and his hand made a quick karate chop in the air, "This is *Hance,* and it's only the first of the Big Drops."

Adam responded to the karate chop by springing to another boulder and adopting a Ninja pose. As we giggled at the sight, Al pointed downstream and raised his voice even higher over the roar of the rapid. "That's the Inner Gorge down there. *Sockdolager, Horn Creek, Granite, Hermit, Crystal, Lava* . . . you ever hear of Lava Falls, the steepest navigable rapid in North America?"

"Sure," Troy answered nonchalantly, "you told us all about it at Westwater."

This time Al pointed to the sky. A ribbed layer of high, thin clouds was racing toward us from downstream. "Add weather," Al said. "I think the weather's gonna change— think about that. This is October we're talking about, and when it rains, you're gonna freeze. Late October and no wetsuits—you have no idea what it can be like down here. So far it's been a picnic. It's October, folks, no commercial trips running anymore and hardly any private trips, either.

No one to rescue you if you get into trouble. You haven't run even *one* of the Big Drops yet."

The Big Drops. The name alone made me feel sick.

"Thanks a lot for the advice," Troy said. "Now butt out."

Al gave Troy a quick appraisal, and shook his head. "So you're the leader, Troy. That's what I'd guessed. Your idea to begin with?"

"Mine," Pug declared.

"No, mine," Rita said.

"Who's rowing the gear boat?"

"Troy is," I said, "—and he hasn't had any trouble."

Troy shot me an approving glance, while Al gave me an annoyed look, a look that indicated he'd expected better of the professor's daughter, and said, "Well, I'm rowing through Hance. I'm joining you guys whether you like it or not. I can get you through Hance and the rest in one piece."

Troy laughed. "Hey, don't worry about us."

"These are my boats, Troy. My gear. You don't have the experience to be running this river. Aside from being responsible for your safety, I have my investment to protect."

I never thought about that. Al wasn't exactly wealthy, and he had an awful lot tied up in all this gear.

Everybody turned silent for a minute and looked out at the rapid. It was ferocious. The sun was off us, the wind was whistling up the canyon, and it was turning cold fast. "Better camp here tonight," Al said. "If we have trouble in Hance, there's no recovery all the way through Sockdolager and below. No camp until Grapevine."

It was odd hearing the names of everything, and hearing about what was waiting for us downriver. It made everything scarier, but I'm sure that's what Al had in mind.

We made camp, and Al insinuated himself back in the middle of us. He helped unload the boats, set up the kitchen, and start dinner. It gave us a lift physically, but it was highly strange to have him there among us after so much time by ourselves. We whispered a lot. Troy and I were suddenly as close as ever. Everybody was asking what Troy was going to do. Troy was saying we'd get together later without Al and talk about it.

As we lined up for the green chili casserole, Al was right there with plate and fork along with the rest of us. Pug was getting really uptight, trying to use his bulk to keep Al from advancing too close to the casserole, all the while appealing to Troy with his eyes. Finally Pug said, "Hey, Troy, are we going to let this guy eat our food?"

I remembered my father saying that even the fiercest tribes in the Sahara Desert would share bread and salt with their enemies. Troy's and my eyes met. He was uncertain. "There's plenty," I whispered.

" 'Course we're going to feed him," Rita said, jumping up and grabbing the serving spoon, dishing out a healthy portion. "It's not like you're going to starve, Pug."

Al got this quizzical look on his face, like he was almost enjoying the situation.

We ate for a couple minutes in silence, looking around at each other and taking in how much Al had changed everything.

"Good green chili," Al said. "One of my favorite meals."

DOWNRIVER

Adam dragged the rocket box he was sitting on over next to Al and sat down. "So how'd you know we'd be right here right now?" he asked with a conspiratorial wink. "Satellite photography? You got the CIA on our case?"

Al shrugged. "I saw you from the tower on the rim."

"Through a telescope?" Pug asked eagerly.

"That's right."

"I knew we should've mooned 'em!"

"Too bad," Al remarked dryly. "An opportunity for greatness lost forever, eh? So I took off down the New Hance Trail. I knew you'd have to pull out to scout Hance."

Adam whistled his admiration. "Bet you had to hustle."

"Look, guys, I appreciate the meal, but I have to wonder—have you been rationing your food?"

Nobody answered. If anything, we were borrowing from supplies intended for future meals. Rita especially liked to "spice things up," and Pug was always nibbling. I even wondered if he nibbled at the food that was hard to count, like dried fruit and trail mix, in the middle of the night.

"Looks like you haven't. Let's see . . . ten days of food, and you're at Mile Seventy-six and on your sixth day. You aren't quite a third of the way through the canyon. . . ."

"A third of the way?" Rita gasped.

Mile Seventy-six, I thought. I looked around. Everybody was shook up.

"Looks like you're in for some fasting."

"Troy," Rita said, "what made you think we could do this trip in ten days?"

In my mind I was inventorying the dwindling food

113

supplies in the rocket boxes. "We have plenty of rice," I said.

"It's all relative," Al said. "When Major Powell and his men were here at Hance in 1869—they were the first—they were living on coffee grounds and rancid bacon."

Al looked around, and he could see he had us plenty worried.

"Are you taking off at Diamond Creek, Troy, or Lake Mead?"

"Figure it out when we get there," Troy mumbled.

Al reached into his pack, pulled out a waterproof mile-by-mile guide to the Grand Canyon, and began turning back the pages. "Let's see—Hance is at Mile 76, the Diamond Creek road's at 225 and Pierce Ferry's at 280. Of course if we go all the way to Pierce, the last forty miles, I suppose you know, is on Lake Mead, even though it still looks like river on the guide. No current in there—did you arrange for a motorboat to pull you out?"

"We'll deal with it when we get there," Troy said tiredly.

"Could I see that guide?" I asked.

I started paging through the guide. It was a gold mine of information, not only rating all the rapids and showing all the camps, but with sections about the geology, all the plants and animals of the canyon, the history of river running in the Grand Canyon, even a chart on the "daily tides" so you could predict at a certain mile on the river when high and low flows would reach you. "Look at this, Star!" I exclaimed. As chance would have it, I'd happened on a photograph of the big cavern where we'd braided Rita's hair. "We camped right here—it's called Redwall Cavern. Oops, it says no camping allowed."

Al was shocked. He was looking at us like we were crazy—bigger fools than he'd even given us credit for. "You don't mean to tell me that you don't have a mile-by-mile guide?"

"We make it up as we go," Adam said proudly. "We make up our own names for things. This camp, for example, we'll call 'Camp Where Big Al Brings Book Down from Mountain.' "

"Wait a minute, you have to be kidding. You really don't have a mile-by-mile guide?"

"Is there an echo in here?" crowed Rita.

"Did Powell have that map?" Troy said. "I thought you were big on 'wilderness therapy,' Al. Self-reliance and all that. We're doing everything you said. 'Do something great' and all that, remember?"

"Big difference, Troy," Al replied quickly. "Powell was a legend in his own time. You're what I'd call a legend in your own *mind.*"

"*Burn!*" Adam sang. "Chalk one up for old Al."

"What I want to know," Pug said, "—did Heather squeal on us or what?"

Al more or less sighed. "She told me where I could find the van, and about how you were going to run the Grand. I was pretty impressed, believe me. You guys have got more imagination than sense, I'll grant you that. I didn't know if I was more angry or worried. No group's ever taken off on me like that before. Individuals, yes, but never a group acting together."

"We're a dastardly crew, all right," Adam said. "Did you tell the cops and the Park Service on us?"

Al hesitated for a moment, then said, "I thought about it, but no, I didn't."

"How do we know you're not lying?" Troy asked him.

"Well, have you seen any evidence that the Park Service knows you're down here?"

When nobody replied, Al said, "I just want to tag along, row my boat, and see you safely through. Believe it, you need me. I'm not going to be a bother, other'n seeing that you abide by the park rules."

We were all done eating, and Pug was up scraping out whatever of our casserole stuck to the sides of the Dutch oven. Adam handed his blue scorpion-home over to Al. "Care for a chocolate?"

I held my breath as Al took the soap case in his hand. He knew it was some kind of a test. He looked around, trying to read us, and then he opened it up.

He opened it up a little way, peeked inside, and saw the scorpion. Very deliberately, he snapped the case shut and handed it back to Adam. His face flushed in a hurry—he was pretty mad. Just as quickly he regained control. "That's very funny," he said. "That's the slender scorpion you've got there, Adam. There are six varieties of scorpions in the canyon, and that's the only deadly one."

Pug laughed derisively. "Sure it is, Al."

Al nodded toward me. "Key it out in the guide book. Over fifty deaths in Arizona alone. It's much more dangerous than a rattlesnake bite. It's got a nerve poison, and you can go into shock real quick."

I was looking it up. Everything he said was there, in the

DOWNRIVER

guide, including pictures of the six scorpions. Sure enough, Adam's was the deadly one. Sixty-five deaths in Arizona over a twenty-year period. It said that the really nasty-looking one, the giant hairy scorpion, was relatively harmless.

"So, Rita," Al said, seizing the initiative, "where'd you get the cut, and who stitched you up?"

She looked over at Adam. "I got it from a falling meteor, and a veterinarian sewed me up." She gave Freddy a poke. Everybody was laughing.

Al could see it was an inside joke. His reaction made me think how pathetic his whole position was. Everything at this point was an inside joke. It's hard enough for a man in his forties to boss around a bunch of teenagers in the first place, and then they take off and make a fool of him.

Al kept trying to hang in there. "Looks like he did a good job of it too. I haven't heard from you, Freddy—what are you up to, besides practicing medicine?"

"Runnin' the Grand Canyon," Freddy said with a shrug. He always seemed to avoid Al back at base camp. He seemed to distrust authority as much as any of us. After what had happened to his father, I could understand why.

"How about you, Star?"

"I'm with them," Star said simply, and you could tell that was all she was going to say. I was proud of her. Even though she wasn't as loud as most, she was one of us and she felt okay about it. I did too. I thought how well we'd done on an unknown river, coming through one tight spot after the next and doing it in style. Still, as Al said, we hadn't run the Big Drops yet. . . .

After it got dark, Troy asked Al to leave. "Take a long

walk," Troy said. "We've got a lot to talk about. We'll yell when you can come back."

Al stood up, zipped his jacket, and grabbed his knit cap out of his pack. "Fine," he said. "Just remember what's at stake here. You guys need me. This ain't no disco—this is the Grand Canyon."

"Beat it," Pug said.

"Tell us if you find the disco," Rita called after him.

We pulled in close and had our huddle. Everybody was so pumped up. "Let's tie him up and leave him behind," Pug said.

"Ah yes," Adam sang. "The old honey and red ants ploy. Or how about tie him up and take him along—more possibilities."

"Keel-haul him!" Pug shouted, as he unleashed his pirate blade and stuck it between his teeth.

"How about if we let him run along the side?" Adam continued. "It would be interesting to see if he could keep up. Can't you picture him climbing up the gorge, leaping across chasms, plunging into the river? Al could do it, if anybody could. . . ."

"How about," Rita suggested hopefully, "how about if we keep him on the condition that he does all the cooking and all the dishes, unloads the boats, puts up our tents and all that?"

"Good idea," Adam said brightly. "We'll make him wear a little apron. Maybe we can improvise a maid's outfit from yucca leaves and driftwood. We'll send him out for fast food."

Freddy, I noticed, was hugely enjoying all this. Troy, however, was too busy thinking and was missing most of

DOWNRIVER

Adam's routine. "How about if we brainwash him," Adam went on, "turn him into a—"

"All right, all right," Troy said, waving his hands. "We have to think. Will somebody pour ice water on this guy's brain?"

Adam gave a snappy salute. "Sorry Captain, lost my mind for a moment. Waiting for instructions, sir."

"The question is, do we need him or not?" Troy said soberly. "Do we need him to get through the rapids? Does anybody want him around otherwise?"

"No way," Rita said. "It's more fun without him, no question about it."

Troy picked up a little stick and started jabbing it in the sand. "I'd say we're agreed on that—we'd rather see if we can get through the canyon on our own, which is what we set out to do. Not taking Al back in, that's not a crime, is it? Whatever we've done, we've already done. Look, you guys, we decided to run it on our own. Why should Al showing up change anything?"

"I'm havin' a good time," Rita said. "I don't want to make any deals, if that's what some of you guys are thinking."

"Right on!" said Pug.

Rita was right about me at least. I was suddenly picturing myself in jail, and thinking if we'd let Al join us here, maybe all would be forgiven. But I sure wasn't going to say it out loud, not now, not under Troy's eyes.

"Look, you guys," Troy said. "We don't need him. He wants to scare us into thinking we do, but we can run those Big Drops as well as he could. I say we take off without him in the morning."

"He's gonna be watchin' us close," Rita said.

"If it comes to it, we could push him off the boat."

"Count me out," Freddy said abruptly. "I ain't wrasslin' with Al. Remember who this guy is. He fought in Vietnam, don't you remember?"

Pug whipped out his knife. "We got a persuader."

I was vividly recalling a certain chapter from Pug's biography. I wished we were talking about leaving him behind too.

"I got nothing against Al," Freddy said. "I just want to run the Grand Canyon."

"You can put the toadsticker away now," Troy said to Pug, and then turned to Freddy. "So you'd rather take him along?"

Freddy shrugged. "Can't hurt, can it? Besides, I'm not really sure we can make it through this rapid right here without him, are you?"

"What does he know that we don't?"

"The route, maybe—I sure don't see it, do you?"

"No," Troy said uncomfortably, "but we can pick one and give it our best."

There was a level of tension here we'd never felt before, even though Freddy was trying to keep it low-key. Troy sure didn't want to make another mistake like back at Storm King, when we followed him up the wrong route.

Freddy didn't speak for a bit, then added, "And then what? What if both boats flip? That other bad rapid is only a mile downstream."

"*Al* said it was a mile downstream," Troy said, visibly offended. "That doesn't mean it is."

I thought, wait a minute, Troy, the mile-by-mile guide says it's there too.

Freddy threw up his hands. "It's just what I think. He knows some moves we don't, and more about first aid and rescue. But if you want to try it without him, that's okay with me too."

"You just won't help us with Al," Pug sneered.

"That's right," Freddy said softly.

Troy hesitated, then said grudgingly, "We'll let him on for this rapid, and then we'll see. It's probably not as bad down in the gorge as he said. We can pick when and where we want to ditch him."

· 12 ·

I STAYED UP READING BY FLASHLIGHT LONG after Star fell asleep. I was reading the mile-by-mile guide and learning about the Grand Canyon. The worst rapid we'd done so far was called House Rock, rated an 8, and I figured out it was the one where Troy stood his boat on end. Where the paddle raft flipped and Star took her bad swim was in the Roaring Twenties, which were 5's, 6's, and 7's. Sockdolager, just two miles downstream from Hance, was an 8 or a 9, depending on water levels, and the string of names Al mentioned—Horn Creek, Granite, Hermit, Crystal, and Lava—were pretty much 9's and 10's, depending on the water levels.

Outside in the dark, the rapid thundered even louder than it had in the daytime. I was snug in my sleeping bag, but chills ran down my spine as I paged through photographs of overturned boats in waves bigger than any we'd seen yet, and photographs of boats wrapped around rocks in the middle of the current. I was happy that Freddy had had the courage to speak up about keeping Al on. We were bound to be safer—that was just common sense.

Common sense made me think of Adam. I could hardly believe how little of it he seemed to have. His routines were a delight, but was he for real? The scorpion sure was. I kept waiting to get a glimpse of another side of Adam, one when he wasn't "on stage," but so far he was all jokes and tricks.

I went back to reading about Major Powell and his men. In his journal Powell remarked how he and his men felt "like pigmies, running up and down the sands, or lost among the boulders." I could relate to that. The guide said that three of Powell's men lost hope and tried to hike out of the canyon. They never made it. The next party to try the canyon had two men drown fifteen miles below Lee's Ferry.

In the morning we were subdued and tense. Waking up, I felt like I'd taken a pounding from the rapid already. We stood and listened as Al got us together up on the hill and pointed out our route through Hance. "You guys in the paddle raft, follow me close but not too close. Watch exactly where I enter at the top of the rapid. If you miss by even a foot or two, you'll either wrap on a rock or be sucked into a big reversal."

I glanced over to Troy. He hated this. He really hated it.

Al charted strategy for the rest of our moves all the way through the rapid. It was pretty complicated and would require perfect teamwork. I was going to be paddling along with the others, and so was Troy. Star was going to be Al's passenger in the oared raft.

Al and I were off by ourselves, untying the boats from the small trees by the shore. "I always look around the base of these tammies before I put my hand in there," he said. "Rattlesnake hangout. Probably hibernating already, but you never know."

"What are 'tammies'?" I asked him.

"Tamarisks—these overgrown bushes. They aren't native to North America; they came from Egypt, and spread all over these desert rivers. Say, Jessie, I talked to your dad."

My heart about stopped. "Yes . . ."

"He's really worried."

Good, I thought.

"He was thinking about coming along with me."

I'm sure glad he didn't, I thought. I could just picture that—everybody checking him out. I would have looked like an idiot. "So," I said slowly, "is there a message or what?"

"Well, he's terribly concerned about your safety, but he doesn't want to tell you what to do—he wanted me to tell you he has faith in you."

"Gee, thanks," I said.

"Let's get going," Troy shouted nervously. "Remember, we got miles to cover."

"I have faith in you too," Al was saying.

I wasn't going to let him get to me. It came back fast, that sensation of hanging upside down and looking down a sheer wall for a thousand feet. I snapped, "I wish I could say the same about you."

Then we pushed off. As we paddled through the slow water, following Al's lead toward the edge of the drop, my heart was doing loops. Spumes of white water jetted up from below the brink. Al and Star dropped from sight. The Thunder was deafening—the adrenalin was flowing.

Then we squeezed between two huge boulders and slid over the edge. Our line was perfect and we escaped the two sucking holes on either side, underneath. From then on it wasn't possible to follow Al's lead; there was time only to react to what was happening. We banged off a rock and lost control, went up and over a tall wave, and free-fell into a hole. For five or ten seconds we were held there, surfing. Paddling was useless. We were spun sideways, the downstream side of the boat pitched up in the air, and I felt sure we were going to flip. Troy and I were trying to lunge toward that high side, but all we were doing was flailing.

I glanced back at Freddy and saw that same wild look in his eye that I remembered from Storm King, when my life was in his hands and he was up there on the other end of the rope. His jet-black hair was flying as water boiled all around us, and his dark face shone with that same feral joy and determination. The strength in his paddle, far beyond what you might guess could be marshaled by someone his size, was bracing the boat in the hole and preventing us from flipping. Finally the hole spit us out, and we pinballed through the rest of the rapid. We got sideways in the tailwaves once, but we were so heavy with water we didn't flip.

Al was eddied out below. They'd taken so little water, Star was hardly bailing. We paddled alongside them and Rita reached out for the chicken line that circled their boat. She grabbed it and held the rafts together. Everybody was shouting, retelling our ride. I glanced back to Freddy, and our eyes met. I didn't say anything, but I think he could tell

I knew what he'd done and how much I thought of him.

For a minute, as we celebrated, it seemed as if Al was one of us. *"That* was a Big Drop," he said. "Wild and crazy, eh?"

Somebody hollered, "Look at the walls!" We were in a dark gorge that bristled with thousands of sharp angles.

"The bowels of the earth," Al declared, almost fondly. "The Inner Gorge. Vishnu schist, Brahma schist, Zoroaster granite—this stuff is two billion years old, half as old as the earth. It's so old there's only one-celled fossils in it."

"Thanks for the geology lesson," Troy said sarcastically.

"My pleasure, Troy. Sockdolager coming up. An old boxing term—it means a 'knockout punch.'"

"Sock-doll-a-jer," Freddy repeated.

We had no trouble with Sockdolager either, or Grapevine, which followed. Just terrific rides. I was happy to be back in the paddle raft, even if Troy wasn't. I could tell it wasn't only watching Al work the oars that was torturing Troy: It was the combination of Al having usurped the oars and Troy finding himself one of the crew on Freddy's paddle raft. Troy had fallen from a great height to a lowly place.

In the calm water I got out the mile-by-mile guide and read all I could. It was amazing how much information was packed into its pages.

Troy said as we floated, and not very loud, "We need Al like a fish needs a bicycle. We can do every rapid in this canyon without him."

I started reading to him out of the guide, which annoyed him for some reason. He said, "Put that thing away, would you?"

I pretended I hadn't heard that, and went back to reading silently. Troy was starting to get on my nerves again.

Al eddied out after awhile and waited for us to catch up. I asked him about this Phantom Ranch about five miles down the river that was mentioned in the guide. "Do they really have a snack bar where you can get burgers and malts?" I asked.

That sure grabbed everyone by the ears.

"Yes, ma'am," Al said, "Phantom Ranch. Only a ten minute walk from the river, and the only piece of civilization in the entire canyon. From Phantom it's only nine miles to the Park Headquarters up on the South Rim, in case anybody wants to run up for a steak dinner. There's cabins at Phantom, a little post office, even a telephone."

"I want to write a postcard to my mother," Rita said. "I don't want to talk to her, though—she'll get hysterical."

"Make sure you get your card hand-stamped," Al told her. "The stamp says, 'Carried Out by Mules from the Bottom of the Grand Canyon.'"

We were talking about blitzing full-speed ahead down to Phantom for lunch, but then Al had us stop and take a hike. "Clear Creek's an amazing canyon. Easy walking, great waterfall."

Not everyone came along. Troy and Pug said they weren't interested and would rather hang out at the boats.

Clear Creek would have been pleasant if the sky hadn't clouded over on us. Our feet were freezing as we walked up the shallow stream between the polished, narrow walls. I got to thinking it was a little strange that Al was taking the time for this hike, when he was so concerned about our dwindling food supply and all the river miles to come. The waterfall wasn't nearly as close to the river as he'd suggested but finally we made it.

If the sun had been shining, we could have followed Al' lead and stood under the falls, letting the water massage ou shoulders. But on a day like this you would have to b crazy, which is the diagnosis we gave Al for his condition Star and I followed him around the side of the pool int the chilly grotto behind the falls. He didn't seem to b suffering from the cold at all. "Maidenhair ferns," Al said pointing to the hanging greenery. What a lovely name, thought. I caught Star's eye, and we smiled as we shivered It was a name that would fit into her Tarot world. Ad sunlight, and this would be a place that should be picture on one of her cards.

As we returned to the boats, I saw right away that Tro was pretty down. He and Pug had the lunch box out. "Hey it's way past lunchtime," Troy grumbled. "Let's eat. I would be stupid to wait until Phantom now." Nobody spoke as we ate lightly from trail mix and dried apples. I was so strange having Al there with us. The whole feeling was different. It wasn't our trip any more—*our* trip wa over. I understood Troy's feelings. I felt sad for him, and for all of us.

We floated the narrow gorge between bristling black walls on down toward Phantom, and I paged through the mile-by-mile guide as a diversion. After a few miles Rita yelled and pointed, and I looked downstream to see a foot bridge spanning the canyon. We beached just past it on the right side. There were no people or buildings around, only a trail sign for Phantom Ranch. We got out of the boat and stood around and stretched.

DOWNRIVER

"So where are these cheeseburgers?" Pug said.

"I don't care if we just ate," Rita said. "I'm going to order two burgers and a malt."

"I'd even eat a hamburger," Star said. "Maybe two."

Al was looking around as if he was looking for something, which surprised me. He was supposed to know where everything was.

Then everything started happening at once. A string of men came clattering across the footbridge. We looked up and saw uniforms—a whole lot of park rangers, and at least one policeman.

We looked to Al immediately. He was glancing from us to them and back again, and trying to think fast. It wasn't hard to figure out what was happening: We'd been double-crossed. Al looked distressed—obviously there's been some foul-up in his plans. The troops were late. "Trap!" Troy yelled. "We've been set up! Back in the boats, quick!"

Freddy, in a blur, was already untying our bowlines. Al was looking up the trail to see if his army was going to get to us in time. They were off the bridge and running full tilt now, but we were scrambling for our life jackets and jumping into the boats. Nobody was going to stop and debate about whether to give ourselves up. There's nothing like being chased to make up your mind for you.

Al didn't have that much he could do about it. Pug had already pulled his knife and was keeping Al at bay, covering our retreat like a genuine commando. After years of reading *Soldier of Fortune,* he was having his ultimate fantasy come to life. Adam, meanwhile, was circling Al in a gleeful dance, striking his Ninja poses.

"You tricked us!" Rita screamed at Al, and then she

129

added a string of New York's best obscenities.

Troy was rowing away, and as Pug and Adam backed aboard, we paddled away too.

Al was reaching for our bowline, which was loose on the beach. I gave it a huge jerk and it snapped past his hands.

We were free. We caught the current as all those uniformed men came running down the trail and joined Al at the beach.

"You don't have enough food!" Al shouted.

"Rice!" Rita yelled back. "Thanks for packing all the extra rice!"

"What if the weather turns bad? . . . Don't do it!"

We didn't care. We were pointing back at them and laughing.

· 13 ·

AL AND THE PARK RANGERS AND THE POLICE couldn't chase us very far along the shore. The gorge soon constricted, and a minor rapid whisked us through jagged cliffs of fractured black rock rising vertically from the water on both sides. A glance back gave no hint of the beach at Phantom, the footbridge, or our would-be captors.

We couldn't see up and out to the canyon above the gorge. It did feel, as Al suggested, as if we were in the bowels of the earth. We'd slipped the noose, but a look around at the menacing black rock provided no context for celebration; rather, it set us brooding on the consequences of our bolt for freedom and filled us with foreboding.

It was late afternoon and the daylight was fading. Each of these October days was shorter than the one before, but this one, with the cloud cover, seemed to be closing by the minute. I was once again in the front of Troy's boat, with the paddle raft floating right alongside us. Adam was holding on to our chicken line, keeping the two boats snugged together. The wind was blowing, our feet were blocks of ice in the cold water in the bottom of the boat, and everybody was pulling on sweaters, then rainslickers, to try to ward off the icy waves. "Holy cow!" Rita wailed, "I've never been this cold in my life!"

Rita let her teeth chatter so hard I thought they'd break. I was fretting, thinking how complaining might make her feel better, but it sure didn't make the rest of us feel very good. I thought about telling her to cut it out, but I knew she'd yell at me no matter how I put it. I put my nose back in the mile-by-mile guide, that invaluable gift from our twice-former leader. And what a boon it would be, especially knowing the location of camps and rapids.

I read to everybody about what was coming up, namely Horn Creek Rapid, only two miles downstream. "What's it rated?" everybody wanted to know. "How bad is it?"

Everybody wanted to know, I should have said, except Troy. He seemed pained; he had an attitude about that guide.

"Horn Creek's an eight or a nine, except at low water," I explained. "At low water it's a ten. It says, 'not recommended below ten thousand cubic feet per second.' I guess that would make it into a ten-plus."

"So how much water is ten thousand cubic feet per second?" Rita asked nervously, through her chattering teeth. "How much are we on now?"

"Well, there's five feet of bathtub ring on the shore," I said. "The river's not high, that's for sure. The question is, how low is it?"

"I don't know about the rest of you guys," Adam said,

"but I'm not fond of that 'not recommended' bit. . . . I mean, you don't want to see me cry like a baby, do you? My feet are so cold as it is, they feel like they might break off. Wouldn't this be a lovely evening for a swim?"

Star started to protest Adam's pessimistic imagery, but he stopped her. "Star, don't even say what I think you're going to say—it's bad luck to say something is bad luck. What do you guys say we think about camp?"

I looked to the map, and was happy to report that the guide listed a small camp above Horn Creek Rapid on the right. Everybody was relieved.

"We'll take it," Adam said. "Make a reservation. Give them Troy's credit card number."

That brought a smile to Troy's face. "Fine with me," he said.

I watched the right side for that camp, and then both banks, as we picked up the hiss of the River Thunder downstream. The cliffs continued to skyrocket out of the river on both sides, and there wasn't a bit of sandy beach as far down as I could see into the twilight.

On and on we drifted, as the Thunder increased. "Hug the right side," Troy told the others. "We can't afford to miss that camp."

"If there's a place to perch, we'll take it," Rita agreed. "I'm scared. Let's paddle upstream, guys. I changed my mind about calling my mother."

Rita wasn't the only one who was thinking about paddling upstream. I'd already considered it, and realized that paddling upstream here would be about as difficult as time travel. It's a one-way river, I thought. Against this kind of current, we couldn't gain twenty feet even if we threw all the gear out and all seven of us paddled like maniacs. Pulling the boats upstream along the shore was an impossibility as well. Given the cliffs, there was nowhere to walk.

The heartless river gods turned up their Thunder and turned down the daylight. Closer and closer we drifted toward the murky brink of Horn Creek Rapid, and still no camp, no beach, not even a sliver of sand. The cliffs stood back a bit on the right side, but the bank was steep and lined with boulders. What was wrong? Where was the camp that the guide promised? Could high water have washed it away? Maybe some things change from one year to the next. What did we know? I handed the guide to Troy and let him scour it too. This had to be a Big Drop, it had to be Horn Creek Rapid from the awful sound of it and the nearing horizon line on the water, the jets of white water spurting up from below. Everybody on the other boat was standing up and looking this way and that for the camp that wasn't there. We shouted back and forth, and there was panic in our voices. "Where's camp, Jessie?" Troy asked anxiously, as he tossed the guide back to me and pulled at the oars. "You said there was a camp."

Blame it on me, I thought. That's not going to help anything, Troy.

A few seconds went by, with everybody watching Troy and waiting, as we drifted even closer to the brink. What was he waiting for? Panic ripped through us as it appeared we might lose the chance to get to shore, and drift over the edge without even scouting. "Right side!" Troy yelled at last. "Tie up!"

I stumbled around among the boulders and tied off our bowline. I looked up from another pair of hands on another rope to see Star's face, numb and blue. "So much for Jessie's camp on the right side," Troy was announcing sarcastically. I couldn't believe he was doing that. Everybody kind of looked away. It was embarrassing. It was all I could do to keep from calling him out about it right there—I was thinking, if I let him get away with it now, it's going to get worse. "Let's think about what we're going to do, Troy," I suggested instead.

"Scout the rapid, I guess. We got sucked into this because of that river guide of yours."

I couldn't take it anymore. "Look, Troy, it's not my fault, okay? Probably there used to be a beach here and they washed it away, jerking the river up and down all the time with their stupid dam."

In silence we picked our way through the slick boulders on the right side, to the brink, to take a look at Horn Creek Rapid. It was simply terrifying. A short big drop with teeth, the top was studded with rocks, which funneled the only passable water into an explosive fall and chaos below—huge waves recoiling on themselves, waves attacking from both sides, and deep, boiling suckholes. "Ten-plus," Rita rasped.

Freddy asked, "What does the guide say about camps downstream?"

I was so scared, teeth chattering too, that I didn't even realize I had the guide in my hand or that he was talking to me. "Jessie, could I see the map?"

He turned a page over and scanned downstream. "What are you looking for?" I asked.

"Camps downstream."

"You don't really think we can run this tonight, do you?"

"If we do, I'd like to know if there's any camps coming up, any beaches where we could recover if we have trouble."

Adam and Pug were looking over Freddy's shoulder. "There's a small camp, theoretically, about a mile down," Adam said. "And another theoretical small camp a mile after that, and then comes Granite Rapid, which is either an eight or a nine."

"Would you guys hurry up and decide what you're doing?" Rita said. "It's going to get dark, or haven't you noticed?"

"Lemme see that thing," Troy said, almost shouting over the roar of the rapid. He was standing atop the highest boulder, and Adam handed the river guide up to him.

In one swift motion Troy tossed the guide out into the current streaming toward the lip of the rapid. Disbelieving, helpless, we watched it float over the brink and disappear in the white water.

We were stunned. No one said a word. No one could have thought of such an act. I couldn't begin to calculate what the loss might mean, but I felt sick to my stomach. We were all looking at each other, totally bewildered, and sneaking glances at Troy, whose eyes were locked on the rapid. I looked back to Freddy, but he'd turned inward.

Troy, I thought, I don't really know you at all.

I can't remember ever being more scared than I was at that moment.

Then Troy spun around. His eyes were flickering. "We were doing a lot better without that thing," he said. "We never assumed anything. We used our own resources."

No one wanted to counter him. He was burning up with energy. We were all shivering and shaking. Freddy scrambled to the top of a boulder and studied the rapid. "Hey, whadda we do, Troy?" Rita said, jogging in place and hugging her sides. "Just tell us what to do."

"*Run* it."

"I have a bad feeling about this one . . . ," Adam said.

It was spooky, hearing these sentiments from Adam. He'd do anything.

"We're gonna flip," Pug concluded.

"Don't *say* that," Star objected, practically sobbing.

Rita stuck her face in Star's. "We're only gonna *die*. How's that for imaging?"

"Cut it out, everybody," Troy said. "Freddy, what do you think? If we can run it, it would be stupid to huddle in these rocks all night long."

"It could be raining in a few hours," Freddy said. "Somebody might get sick. I think we can run it, but we better go quick and find camp before it gets dark."

I couldn't believe what I was hearing. I pointed to that ugly rapid and practically screamed at the two of them. "Look at it, will you! Are you guys out of your minds? What if both boats flip? Who's going to live through the night?"

"Great," Troy said. "Get hysterical, Jessie."

There was no sense appealing to him. "Freddy," I pleaded, "I'm not hysterical, I'm trying to be rational."

"Come up here," he said, and extended his hand. I let him pull me up beside him on the boulder. "It's not as bad as it looks, really. We stay on the inside of the tongue as we enter, and then, look, there's good water moving through all the way down. We stay on that line—no trouble."

I could begin to see the route. "Are you sure . . . ?"

"This water level's okay. We aren't going to flip."

"You guarantee it?"

He smiled and rolled his eyes. "No guarantee."

Troy got everybody up on the rocks and pointed out the run that he and Freddy saw, talked strategy, and then we all scrambled, slipping and sliding, through the mossy rocks back to the boats. Shaking with the cold, I tugged at the cinches of my life jacket and tightened them up as much as I could. Star was struggling to do the same, but her fingers wouldn't cooperate. "Here, Star," I said, and helped her out. "Good luck," I whispered.

"Let's go, Jessie," Troy called nervously. "I want you to ride as far forward as you can, and hold that front end down." He was already in his seat and had the oars in his hands.

Despite all my misgivings I was stumbling around in the rocks, untying the bowline, hearing and seeing and feeling everything through a numbing fog. I couldn't have felt any less in focus. *Is this how it happens?*

"Ready, Freddy?" Troy was saying.

"Just a sec."

Freddy was rigging a piece of rope from one side of the paddle raft, underneath, to the other side. "In case we flip," he was saying to the others, "don't get separated from the raft. Hang on to the chicken line, then pull yourself up this rope and get onto the bottom of the boat."

"Should we rig one of those?" I asked Troy.

"Forget it," he said. "We're losing time. We aren't going to flip, Jessie. Now get in the boat, will you?"

I did. I got in the boat, stowed the bowline, and looked back for Star. She gave me a little wave. "Hang on to those paddles, no matter what," Freddy was telling them. "We can't afford to lose one."

Troy was rowing out into the current. I moved forward in the boat, and spread-eagled my weight against the very front. I tried to wedge my legs into the cracks where the tubes met the floor. Only my face projected above the level of the tubes—there was no way I was going to get blown out of the boat by a big wave. The roar of the rapid intensified, the current picked up. Behind us I heard Adam and Pug chanting, "Horn Creek! Horn Creek! Horn Creek!"

"Hang on, babe," Troy said under his breath, and I felt the boat dropping, dropping, dropping. I couldn't see a thing with all the water pouring over me. The boat filled, just that fast. As the boat bucked and pitched with the pounding, I wondered if I was going to float out of it. I struggled to plant my legs, but just as quickly as it had all happened, it was over, and Troy was yelling, "Bail! Bail!"

I pitched two buckets of water out as Troy struggled in the turbulence to keep the boat off the dark cliff walls, and then I glanced back to check on the paddle raft. "They made it!" I yelled. "Troy, they made it!"

"O ye of little faith," Troy chided.

I bailed and bailed. "That was incredible, Troy! You were awesome! They're all in the boat too—no swimmers!"

"What'd I tell you, Jessie? Now let's find camp."

If I'd never been so scared in my life, I'd certainly never been as relieved.

We found our small camp on the left, a little beach shining in the gloom like a beacon, right where it was supposed to be. Thank goodness it was there: a couple of more minutes on the river and we would have had to run by flashlights.

It was quickly agreed there'd be no dinner this night. Breaking out our warm clothes and putting up tents would about do it for the day. Who cared if we were hungry and freezing—we were alive.

After a while we were all sitting around the gas lantern in a tight circle, warming our hands over the exhaust fumes and rehashing our near-death experience. Everybody had a different slant on it, but Adam, bounding quickly back into form, provided the tour de force of the evening. "Great moments in history!" he shouted, and leaped to his feet. Dancing among the rocks, his face coming in and out of the light cast by the lantern, he would announce a name and then strike a pose, as if he were a statue in a wax museum. "David slaying Goliath with a little rock! . . . Ulysses on the john, thinking up the Trojan horse trick! . . . Caesar assassinated in the senate! . . . King Arthur pulling the sword from the stone! . . . Leonardo opening his first box of crayons! . . . Napoleon attempting to free his hand from his vest! . . . Washington standing up in a boat! . . . And, ladies and gentlemen, *and,* the newly minted Greatest Historical Moment of All Time . . . TROY THROWS THE MILE-BY-MILE GUIDE INTO THE COLORADO RIVER!"

Adam mimicked Troy's body language at that fateful moment with uncanny perfection: He took the invisible guide in his hand, and with that Troy-like look of disdain, reenacted the infamous toss and froze halfway through the follow-through, to the howling cheers of his delighted audience.

Troy was laughing along with the rest of us. Adam, I thought, you've made the tension go away, you've defused the anger. I can see what you're doing, what you're telling everybody: Lighten up—what's done is done. It's time to come back together; our survival depends on it.

Rita wasn't exactly on my wavelength. Brash as ever, she up and said, "Hey, Troy, what is it with maps? You have a map phobia or something? I never heard of that one."

"What do you mean?" Troy said defensively.

"Seriously. Remember back on Storm King? You wouldn't look at the map."

True, I thought. Why is that?

As the moon rose, a ghostly half-moon obscured by the clouds, Troy and I sat by the river, holding hands and talking quietly. "I'm sorry," he said. "I guess I was stressed out."

"So was I," I said. "We have to remember not to turn on each other—when the going gets tough, remember we care about each other, yes?" I squeezed his hand.

"And you'll stick with me, okay? That's all I ask."

I said I would, but as I said goodnight and headed for my tent I was more than vaguely uncomfortable. I would try, but the events of this day would not be so easily forgotten, nor the feeling I experienced as he took the river guide out of my hands. I'd felt I was looking into the face of a stranger. Would I ever fully trust him again?

I joined Star in the tent. She was putting away her Tarot cards. In the light of the candle her face looked ashen, and though she looked away, there was no disguising her distress. "What is it, Star?" I whispered. "Did you just see a ghost, or what?"

"Sort of . . . ," she whispered. "I can't tell you."

"But Star, what's the matter? I really feel the worst is behind us, don't you?"

She wasn't going to tell me what it was, but I begged and pleaded with her. It was spooky. Here eyes were going glassy on me.

"Star," I whispered, "if you care about me at all . . ."

She struggled, and then she said, "I do, Jessie. If you promise to listen to what I say and not take it wrong, I'll tell you. I wouldn't tell anyone else in the whole world, but I'll tell you."

She bit her lip, and then she turned one of the cards faceup. I gasped. It was the Grim Reaper astride a white horse.

"Listen, Jessie, don't say anything, you promised to listen. Death is not to be feared, death is only a transition to another realm of existence, and all of us will die one day. You know that."

"Yes, I can accept that, as long as it's at a ripe old age for both of us."

An ethereal smile played at her lips, and her eyes—they seemed to be looking through and past me. She was floating away; she'd never seemed as loosely tied down.

I took her slender forearm by the wrist. "Star," I whispered, "what question did you ask?"

"I asked if I was going to live through this trip."

"Star, that's not a fair question!"

"Oh? Why not?"

"It's self-fulfilling. It's like a death wish. You're the one

DOWNRIVER

who always says, if you think negatively, you'll produce a negative result, right?"

"I didn't ask if I was going to *die* on this trip, I asked if I was going to be alive at the end. That's positive."

"That's voodoo, Star. I'm sorry, but that's all it is. There's so much pudding in your head, you can't think straight."

Star bowed her head. She wasn't going to defend herself.

"So now you have this curse on your head, this death sentence! What are you going to do, not even try to hang on, and get washed out of the boat? Accidentally walk over the edge of a cliff? What?"

She looked up brightly. "Jessie, you still don't understand. I can do my best. I can be cheerful. I can try to be a better person than I ever have before. I just have to be ready for a transition, that's all."

I took her by both wrists and looked her in the eye. "Star, I tell you what: I'm keeping an eye on you. You aren't going anywhere without me."

"I want you to remember me, Jessie, whenever you hear the song of the canyon wren. That's going to be me singing, singing just for you."

"No way," I said. "A canyon wren is a canyon wren. That's what I believe. I want you to be you. I think you're really great, Star."

She smiled painfully. "Thanks for the vote of confidence. I really appreciate it."

"Star, you're . . . you're like a sister to me, the sister I never had. . . ."

"Same here, Jessie," she said dreamily. "I know. These days . . . despite everything . . . they're the best of my life."

My eyes filled with tears.

143

"It's okay, Jessie, don't feel sorry for me. Let's get some sleep."

Star snuggled down into her sleeping bag and fell silent.

In the morning it was cloudier yet: A thicker layer had come in under the high clouds as we slept. I ate my breakfast ration, my one packet of hot cereal, in the general silence. It was going to be a chilly day, and we were in for three Big Drops, as I remembered them from the river guide. Granite Falls, Hermit, and Crystal. Maybe it wasn't a coincidence that the worst rapids were found in the most sinister-looking stretches of the canyon. I looked up and down the river at the black walls, and I remembered for a moment the friendly reds and whites of the cliffs in the upper canyon. I remembered the amber hue of Freddy's miracle fountain, the *sipapuni* by the River of Blue. Gone are the days, I thought. So long gone that our frolic in the sun seemed a distant memory. As I looked up and down the gorge at the tortured black rock, Star's premonition came to mind, and a chill ran through me.

"A penny for your thoughts," Troy said. "Join you for breakfast, such as it is?"

"Sure," I said. I was pleased to have the company. And his blue eyes were warm again, steady. His beard growing in, blond peppered with red, accentuated the old charm that had returned to his smile.

"Well?" he said.

"Just wondering what the day will bring."

"I love river-running, Jessie, I really love it. I love moving water. I love running this big water more than anything I can remember."

"More than surfing?"

He smiled broadly. "I can't knock surfing, but these waves, they're something else."

"You haven't flipped yet—haven't had any trouble at all."

"Where's some wood?" he asked with a laugh, and lunged for a piece of driftwood, almost spilling his oatmeal. "I'm knockin' on it, I'm knockin'."

I was laughing too, and then I was hearing something strange, not having any idea at first what it might be. Pug and Adam were yelling and pointing. It was the unmistakable *chop-chop-chop* of a helicopter. I looked up to see two of them buzzing down the gorge.

We all stood silent for a moment as they flew past, only a couple hundred feet above the water, right down the middle of the gorge. The sound ricocheting off the walls was unbelievably loud. We could see the helmeted men inside looking at us.

"They're after us!" Adam shouted. "The plot thickens!"

"Where's my rocket launcher?" Pug thundered. "Oh, for a couple of Stinger missiles!"

"My, my," Troy said softly, standing next to me. "No place for them to land, is there? That's too bad."

They buzzed us three times, and then they left.

"Heli-*cop*-ters," Rita called them.

· 14 ·

IT WAS AMAZING HOW HIGH OUR ENERGY level shot up with the arrival of those helicopters. Our quiet, brooding camp came alive like a nest of fire ants stirred with a stick. Rita and Pug were still shaking their fists at the skies after the helicopters had disappeared downstream. Without anyone calling us together, we all congregated around Troy, and almost everybody was talking at once. "What now?" Rita insisted.

"Hold everything, and I'll show you what," Adam said. He darted away toward his tent, rifled through his dry bag for something, and dived inside the tent with it. A minute later he emerged a whirling Ninja, triumphantly garbed in black, hooded and masked, and fought his way to us through imaginary assailants. I saw him wince in pain as he sprang from a boulder; he must have taken a hit from one of his many enemies. He even had a samurai sword slung around his back.

DOWNRIVER

He circled us, jabbing and kicking, as we cracked up. Only the darting eyes of the Ninja showed. Gone was the reassuring head of curly hair and the omnipresent grin that proclaimed Adam's motto: "It's all a game."

Everybody was laughing, even Star, who was under a death sentence.

When Adam finally slowed to as near a standstill as he ever gets, Pug said, "Lemme see that thing," and he pulled Adam's sword from its scabbard. "Wait a minute," he said, hugely disappointed. "It's not real."

Sure enough, it was a rubber sword.

The Ninja said, "That's in case I have to fall on it one day."

"So, Adam," I said, "you carried this outfit all the way down the river and waited until now to pull it out. That must have taken quite a bit of restraint."

"Hey, *they* brought out the choppers. No more Mr. Nice Guy."

"I love this," Rita said. "If my friends in New York could see me now."

We held a brief council of war. "If we don't camp at a spot where they can land a helicopter," Troy said, "how are they going to catch us?

Back in our tent Star and I got dressed all over again after thinking how cold we'd been the day before. This time we started with our long johns. It's always much colder out in the boats, over the water, than it is on shore. As we'd discovered the day before, when the sun isn't shining it makes all the difference in the world. We struck the tent and packed our dry bags, leaving our yellow rainslickers out where we could get to them. I'd been thinking hard, and

147

while I still had the chance I took hold of Star and looked her in the eye. "Star," I said, "I've been remembering another one of your Tarot readings: a beautiful girl pouring water, in front of a ring of stars. I asked you what it meant, and you said 'hope and inspiration.' You promise me you'll image that reading today, with all your heart?"

She seemed like she was going to cry. "I will, Jessie, I promise. Thanks."

"Star, maybe I don't take it as far as you do, but I really do believe in positive thinking. I could sure use a lot more of it myself."

We looked up to see Adam, still in Ninja regalia, limping over to us. "Jessie," he said, "I have a little problem." He leaned back and lifted the sole of his right foot, revealing a nasty puncture wound.

Star and I winced. He had a puncture under the arch, half the diameter of a dime.

"How'd you do it?" Star asked.

"Stepped on a little stick barely under the sand, is all I can figure."

"While you were playing Ninja. You came down pretty hard on that stick, I bet."

"Sorry, *Mama-san*. I was a bad boy, eh?"

"You were a bad little Ninja. Star, would you get the first aid kit? We better clean it up and try to bandage it, but it's a shame we can't keep it dry. It'll be just about impossible for it to heal, being wet all the time."

Our wounded Ninja sighed. "Just another experience in life. . . ."

"Well, if you don't take care of it, we might have to amputate with that sword of yours."

"I'll be looking forward to that. I'll have the foot bronzed as a memento of the trip."

A half hour later we were on the river again. "Troy, no getting us wet today," I joked.

"Yeah, right," he answered absently. I knew he had a lot to think about. He hadn't fully recovered from the day before, nor had I for that matter. I wished I had the guide, so I could read up some more on Granite Falls, Hermit, and Crystal. They were all highly rated Big Drops, and they were all coming up in short order just a few miles down. Granite and Hermit weren't rated higher than 9, but Crystal, if I remembered right, was rated a 10 at all levels but one, and I couldn't remember if that was at low or high water. Crystal, the guide said, was no more than a riffle until 1966. Then, in one event, the rapid was created overnight when the side-canyon there flash-flooded and created the most feared rapid on the river, along with the notorious Lava Falls.

As we approached a minor rapid, Troy hollered back, "Read 'n' run!" and we started down the tongue as I prayed in vain for a dry ride. The first healthy wave put enough water in the boat to start my feet freezing. I bailed the bottom as dry as possible once we passed through the tail-waves, but the damage was done. Behind us the paddle raft made a flashy fashion statement in their yellow slickers. "Four yellow ducks led by a Ninja," I remarked to Troy.

Troy and I were also wearing our slickers. For the moment I felt warm, except for my feet. I wondered if Adam was already soaked. Maybe he can tolerate it, I thought—his fires are always burning so brightly, and paddling helps you to stay warm. I wondered if Freddy's feet were cold.

"Troy," I said, "Do you think Al was in one of the helicopters?"

"Don't know."

"I was looking, but with their helmets I couldn't tell."

"Who cares about Al?"

"Did you ever think he would trick us like he did? I never thought of it for a second. Why did he even hike in at Hance? Why didn't he hike in at Phantom?"

"He knew we'd scout Hance. He was afraid we'd blow by Phantom. He had to make sure we'd stop there."

"Of course . . . But if he intended to stop us at Phantom, why didn't he just talk with us about it and make a deal or whatever?"

Troy looked at me as if he couldn't believe how naive I was. "Control," he answered coldly. "It would've burned him to negotiate with us—the guy's used to being a dictator. And Jessie, it really aggravates me to have you keep bringing Al up. Especially today. I wish you'd give it a rest."

Troy had an ugly tone in his voice. I was about to suggest he lighten up, but then I realized for a moment what it must feel like to have Granite, Hermit, and Crystal in front of him. No wonder he was uptight.

Maybe the way Troy can row these huge rapids so well is subconscious, I thought. It must take total self-confidence, especially being so new at it. If you ever lost your nerve going into one of those Big Drops, you couldn't function at all. Give him some support, I told myself. He'll need it shortly.

I stood up to do some stretches. "We're going to have a great day of river-running," I said. "We're still out here on our own, running the Grand Canyon and doing fine."

A trace of a smile crossed his face, but the tension lingered.

A minute later he reached forward, clasped my shoulder, and gave me a strained smile. "Just go with the flow, okay, Jessie?"

We began to hear the hiss of a Big Drop downstream, and the current began to die out. Once again we found ourselves on one of those ominous stretches of slow water. "What's with this lake?" Adam called, tongue in cheek.

"Granite Falls," Rita announced, loudly naming the coming attraction. "Holy cow! I wonder why it's called a falls?"

After a while, our boats rounded a bend together, and the Thunder turned up exponentially. Ahead of us, maybe two hundred yards down, was the brink. As we all started looking around for where to scout, Freddy said, "Helicopters."

We heard nothing, but pretty quickly we saw what he was talking about: On the left side, where we would have to scout, the two helicopters were parked, and four men stood on a high point above the beach looking at us. I quickly reconfirmed that there was no chance for us to scout Granite Falls on the right side. It was all cliff over there. They've got us, I thought, almost relieved. They know we'll have to scout Granite. Game's over.

We moved toward river left, to keep the gathering current on the right from sweeping us toward the edge. Safely on still water between the current and the eddy moving back upstream, we could hover and consider our position. At first people were talking loudly, especially Pug and Rita, but Troy told us to keep our voices down—the men on the shore might be able to hear. "One of 'em's Al," Pug said in a stage whisper. "I'm sure of it."

Troy said, "Let's not think about them, let's think about us. They don't have us, you know. Only if we paddle in to that beach and give ourselves up. Is that where we want to be, five minutes from now? With *them?* Think about what fun that's going to be, and think fast."

"We'll probably never see each other again," Rita said. "And we were having such a good time. I don't know about you guys, but I'm not ready to quit, no way. I don't scare that easy."

I started thinking about consequences. I'd thought about them before, but this was so immediate. What were they going to do with us if we gave ourselves up now? What were they going to do if we didn't? "Maybe we should paddle in closer," I said. "We could talk to them?"

I was thinking, maybe we could still cut a deal, but I didn't say it.

Troy wasn't too happy with me. "What about? Are we going to believe what they tell us? Remember how Al tricked us before? They'll do whatever they're going to do. And they'll try to scare us about this rapid. They'll say we can't run it."

"Live free or die," Adam chanted. "Old Japanese saying."

Pug declared, "I'm havin' the best time of my life."

"Can we run it?" I asked.

"Let's ask Star," Rita teased. "She can see the future. Star, what do you think? Do you see us flying out in the helicopters or floating out in the boats?"

"I don't want to fly out in a helicopter," Star said. I was amazed she knew her mind so well, but then, she was prepared to die. "I love the river, and I want to stay with the rest of you for as long as I can. But don't do anything just because I say so."

Troy was pleased. "Freddy, how 'bout you?"

Freddy said, "I don't mind livin' on rice. There's a lot of canyon I haven't seen yet."

I remembered back to the van, when Troy had asked if we were up for the Grand Canyon. It had all hinged on Freddy. Once again, that seemed to be the case. I sensed how misleading it was to be asking Freddy—he was so different from the rest of us. Freddy was the only one, I knew now, the only one who had much of an idea in the first place what we might be getting into, and how bad it could get. He was raised out in the elements on the continental divide. I surveyed the lowering clouds. What about the rest of us? The clouds were darker than they'd been a half hour before. Freddy, I realized, was only speaking for himself; he'd never pretended otherwise. He was assuming that we all were looking out for ourselves. It was a scary thought.

"Let's run it," Freddy said. "It's not a ten, anyway."

Livin' on rice, I thought, that's us—*livin' on rice and adrenalin.*

We circled back upstream on the eddy, and then made for the current that was flowing into the right side of the rapid. The men on the shore were waving their arms, beckoning for us to come in, but we were committed now to Granite Falls. I felt like a wildwoman. "Wil-der-ness ther-a-py!" I yelled at the top of my lungs. My heart was going berserk. Troy was standing up on his seat and scouting. The men were running for a vantage point close to the rapid, now that they could see we were going to run it.

Behind us Freddy was standing up on top of the load in the center of the paddle raft, but he wasn't as close to the edge yet as we were.

"Good water down the right," Troy hollered back. "Rocks center and left. Watch where I enter—stay off the cliff! Looks nasty!"

A second later I could see down the rapid as well. Nasty is right. We were heading for the gut of the rapid, a long dropping succession of enormous waves on a thin line between the rocks in the center and the side-waves exploding off the cliff on the right. Over my shoulder I saw Troy in his glory, rowing the big water in the Grand Canyon of the Colorado, and rowing like he was born to it. *"Downriver!"* I yelled. I braced as torrents of white water poured over and into the boat, and I was instantly soaked to my skin. To the left, I saw Al's face—all eyes—for the briefest of moments, a stone's throw away.

My awareness turned to the cliffs on our right, too close I thought, rushing by so fast and so close I thought certain we'd be dashed against them. Whenever a wave recoiling off the cliff threatened to turn us over, I could feel the boat cock to face it, and we stayed upright. It was over fast. At the bottom we squeezed barely to the right of a hole that would have flipped us, and rode up and down the tall tailwaves.

I rejoiced to see that Freddy's boat had come through as well, with no swimmers. Troy was standing and pointing back upstream, laughing. I spotted the four men, tiny figures now, atop boulders along the shore at the head of the rapid.

After several miles of flat water we neared Hermit, and the helicopters hovered above us. As it turned out, Hermit was easy to scout from the river. Troy stood up and yelled, "Read 'n' run!" and that's what we did, with a perfect run down a roller coaster of huge waves. Hermit wasn't scary at all, just good clean fun, and we were sure enjoying having the audience. "Those guys are probably up there writing songs about us," Adam said, as our boats floated side by side toward Crystal. "The legendary River Pirates—'They never will scout and they never show fear.'"

We ran another rapid that we knew couldn't be Crystal—Crystal was a 10. Then we floated again in tandem, holding the boats together. We began to hear thunder, rolling thunder, booming its way up the canyon from the blackening clouds downstream. As soon as the first lightning bolt struck, the helicopters turned and fled upriver. Pug launched imaginary rockets at the fleeing enemy, while Rita and Adam did a victory dance in the front of the paddle raft. Troy was laughing. "Looks like our friends can't take a little weather."

Looking downstream, I could see a wide band of quartz angling from the river and running skyward through the black rock of the gorge. The next moment I couldn't see the bright band at all, or even the gorge. A dark wall of rain was marching up the canyon.

We couldn't see Crystal when we got there, but we could sure hear it down around the bend, waiting in its lair and growling like all the monsters of mythology combined into one. We got out of the boats and stumbled around in the rain, a steady, heartless, bone-freezing rain. Our minds nearly numb, we made our way down a trail and across a little creek just beginning to turn from clear to muddy red, then picked our way through a field of slippery boulders to the shore of the river. Between us and the cliff wall opposite, the entire flow of the river was pinched into a narrow slot and dropping into a hole so large it seemed out of scale with all the others on the river. The speed and the ferocity of the water stunned me. This was a revelation.

"You could drop a school bus into that hole," Adam said. "And look at the one right below it—nearly as bad!"

From the tops of boulders, we looked and pointed at the awful waves breaking upstream and back into the holes. Troy was talking about how to run it. I tried to picture the route he was describing, and couldn't in my wildest dreams imagine the paddle raft being able to make the moves he was describing, not in this kind of water.

We stood there, Star and I, shivering and shaking and waiting. My feet ached from the cold. Star's hand went to the crystal that hung from her neck. I said, "Let me touch it too."

Freddy wasn't looking at the two huge holes right in front of us, he was looking downstream into the rain. Below the second hole the river widened out into two main channels with a mass of teeth in between—the tops of boulders sticking up from a submerged island.

"Look, Jessie!" Star said, and tugged at my arm. I looked back to the top of the rapid, and saw a red river overtaking the green one we had known. It was an uncanny sight. Just that quickly, the river had turned muddy red.

Freddy scrambled over to us, all happy through chattering teeth. "The *Rio Colorado! 'Colorado'* means red!"

Troy came over, and then everybody. "What do you think, Freddy?" Troy said. His face looked gaunt under that yellow hood, his blue eyes were blazing.

Everybody was watching Freddy. He shrugged. "Looks pretty bad to me."

"But we can run it, right?"

"I'm not so sure."

"Then let me show you the run."

Troy explained his strategy, and Freddy listened. Then Freddy said, "I don't think so. Water's too strong, that hole's too bad. The river's real high right now—lots of power, lots of speed."

Rita was twisting at the hips, hugging herself and blowing her breath into the rain. "So whadda we do, Freddy?"

Again, he shrugged. "There's no reason we can't carry everything around the right side."

"You mean *walk?*" Troy said, unbelieving. *"Portage?* Look how far it is down there."

"It's a lot of work," I said, trying to help out, "but we know we'll get through it safe."

He gave me a look, like he wanted to reach out and hit me. "I can't believe this. Do you guys have any idea how much work that would be? Carrying all our stuff through this boulder field? Look, have we had any trouble so far? How many times have I flipped, tell me that. That's right— *zip, zero, nada.* And I'm going to make it through this one too. Freddy, I can't believe you. You guys have only flipped once, and that was on the first day. I mean, you ran Granite Falls without even looking at it. How do you explain that?"

"I can see this one," Freddy said softly. "I can see how bad it is. And I knew Granite wasn't a ten. This one's a ten, and I can see why."

Troy's face was all red. "Horn Creek was a ten in that stupid book."

"Maybe not at the water level we did it at," I pointed out for the sake of accuracy, and even more because I didn't want to be silenced. I sure didn't want to run Crystal. I'd gladly help Freddy haul the stuff around.

Troy turned on me, on everybody. "Look, we're going to run it, okay."

"Troy," I pleaded, "let's live to run another day."

"Hey, Jessie," Pug said. "If Troy says we're running it, we're running it. What a bunch of wimps. Professor's daughter."

I knew that would come up sometime. I snapped back the last thing I would've guessed, and I'm not even sure why. "I'm proud of my father, Pug. And you get out of my face."

I noticed Adam looking away. This wasn't his idea of a good time.

"So let's get started," Troy said.

"Sorry," Freddy said. "I'm walkin'. If we lose the boats in there, then what happens to us?"

Only Freddy, I realized, only Freddy would have the courage to stand up to Troy. The rest of us were sheep, and had been, all the way down the river.

I looked to Star—she was plenty relieved too.

"We can carry around and be all ready when you run," Freddy said helpfully, "in case anything happens."

"You're so sure we're going to flip," Troy sneered.

DOWNRIVER

"You'd love to rescue us, wouldn't you, Freddy?"

"Wait a minute, Troy," I said. "I want to get something clear. When you say 'us,' I hope you don't mean me. I'm walking."

Troy acted like I stabbed him in the heart or something. "Well, thanks a lot, Jessie, thanks for the vote of confidence. It's good to know who your friends are."

His eyes moved quickly to Pug, then to Adam. "Adam, will you run it with me?"

Adam looked so confused, all out of jokes and looking his age for once, standing there shivering in his suddenly ridiculous Ninja suit. Troy's eyes locked on him; Troy didn't say another word. Adam's face ran the gamut of emotions, and then he ended up with a silly little smile. He drew his sword, brandished it menacingly at the rapid, then bowed.

The rain slackened, and we carried the dry bags through the long boulder field down to the surf-lapped beach near the end of the rapid. Trudging back through the boulders, I remembered how the guide said that Crystal never even used to be a rapid. I mentioned it to Freddy as we walked. "1966," I said. "All these boulders were washed into the canyon in one shot."

Freddy really liked thinking about it. "Those rocks out in the river making those holes," he said. "Think how big they are—the river can't budge them, but they washed down this side-canyon. Pretty neat."

Now all we had to do was carry the paddle raft down. Over in the gear boat, Troy and Adam were making sure everything was secured, and were cinching their life jackets one last time. We didn't talk to them. Obviously they were

159

nervous as could be. Pug stood watching them wistfully, wishing he'd been honored with the invitation that had gone to Adam.

We simply said "Good luck," shouldered the paddle raft, and started our portage. As we crossed the creek and started into the boulder field, we heard a shout above the roar of the rapid and we looked upstream to see a brave, remarkable, idiotic sight: Troy at the oars, his boat picking up speed and approaching the rapid on the glassy incline that fed into the tongue. His Ninja, jumping up and down in the front of the boat, was holding the bowline with one hand, hollering, and waving his free hand like a bronc rider.

We dropped the boat and scrambled for a better view. Evidently they didn't think they needed a rescue boat. More glory without us.

Troy was rowing hard, trying to break off the tongue, trying to pull against that current and break over the big wave on the right side of the tongue. He was working . . . working . . . working . . . but he wasn't making it. At the last second, when he was about to be swept sideways into the jaws of the hole, he spun the boat and took it head on. Amidst the fury of exploding red water, only flashes of them showed. I saw the black Ninja suit hurtling the length of the boat, and I saw Troy's legs directly above the boat, in the air.

A surge lifted the boat up and over the towering wave below the hole. Adam was awash in the river—his hood and mask had been stripped away—and Troy was still in the boat, fighting to regain the oars. The boat dropped sideways into the second hole, and then it flipped.

"Quick!" Freddy yelled, and we jerked the paddle raft over our heads and started stumbling through the boulders. I was breathing hard, falling down, banging my legs. They're going to die, I thought. What in the world are we doing down here?

Halfway down the carry we spotted the gear boat, overturned and pinned against one of the rocks out in the river. It was stuck out there. No sign of Troy or Adam. "Holy mother," Rita said. "Holy mother."

It must have taken fifteen minutes for us to get our boat back in the water. Then we took off, paddling as hard as we could.

We found Troy on the left bank, where he'd crawled out of the water. He was lying face down on the rocks, breathing hard. Pug said, "Buddy, you don't look too good."

"Let's hurry," I said. "We still have to find Adam."

Pug tried to lift Troy. Troy shook him off. "I'm okay, I can get up on my own." He slowly made his way to the paddle raft and got in.

We could have floated right past Adam. Star saw his head barely above the water on the right shore. He had one arm curled around a rock, his body hugging its downstream side. We were all shouting for joy; but when he saw us, he lacked the strength even to smile.

As Pug tied up the boat, we went to pull Adam up on the shore. "My arm," he said. Freddy got in the water with him and came stumbling up the bank with Adam on his back, crying out in pain. As we took him from Freddy and eased him down on a ledge, we could see his right arm dangling useless at his side.

"Dislocated," Adam groaned. "Dislocated my shoulder."

"You're alive," I said. "That's what matters."

"I couldn't get out of the current," Adam was telling Troy. "I was afraid I wouldn't be able to get to shore—couldn't use my arm."

Troy wasn't saying anything. I wondered if he was even hearing Adam.

I tried to look them over for other injuries. Cuts and bruises, lots of those, but I couldn't see anything worse, only Adam's dislocated shoulder. My mind was racing, trying to think if there was anything we could do about his shoulder. I wished I knew more. We scrambled for the dry clothes from the paddle raft. At least we had dry clothes, sleeping bags, and tents with us. I don't think we could've kept those guys alive otherwise. Most of the rest of our stuff was lost under the flipped boat. I knew about hypothermia, knew we had to get them warmed up, and fast. Freddy and Star set up a tent in record time, and we got them into dry clothes and sleeping bags inside the tent.

Before too long the sun came out and the temperature shot up about twenty degrees. Troy and Adam were able to come out of the tent and warm up in the sun.

"I could use one of those helicopters about now," Adam said. I could tell he was in a world of pain. "Where are they when you need them?"

Freddy was thinking about it. He looked doubtful.

"If they don't come soon," Rita said, "we're sunk without that other boat. All our stuff's on it. What are we going to do now?"

"Well, Rita," Adam said, "so much for kicking the Grand Canyon's butt."

DOWNRIVER

* * *

Troy still had nothing to say. He was lying on his back in the sun with his eyes closed.

Freddy said suddenly, "Is the water going down or coming up?"

"It was really low early this morning," I said.

"High water might free our other boat from that rock it's stuck on. We better be ready to catch it if it comes by."

We went to work pushing the paddle raft upstream, two hundred yards at least. We had to make sure we weren't going to get swept downstream and separated from the two guys if we got out in the current chasing the other boat.

And then we waited, as the shadows started to grow across the river.

I thought I saw something moving. A rock maybe, but where there wasn't one before. "Rocks don't move!" I yelled. "Here it comes!"

We paddled out and snagged it, then went back to Adam and Troy.

The good news was that we had our boat back; the bad news was that it was upside down. We could all remember what a struggle it had been to right the much lighter paddle raft when it had flipped. Plus, we were short one man. Adam sure couldn't pull on anything right now. Getting this dead weight turned over seemed like an impossible task to me, but Freddy went to work rigging a pulley system, zig-zagging a long rope through climbing carabiners. Nobody had the slightest idea what he was doing, but he seemed to have a plan, so everybody was happy to just do what he said. And it worked. By degrees we pulled on the free end of the rope and watched the beast of a boat lift little

163

by little out of the water until it stood vertical and flopped down upright. A major victory.

We were losing the day. People were talking about getting some rice cooked. Freddy was looking around a lot, and then he said, "I don't think we should camp here."

"You gotta be kidding," Rita said.

Freddy pointed. "We're at the mouth of a wash. It's clouding up again. The weather might come back—it could flash flood here. We should go downstream and find someplace else."

Troy glared at him. He'd had more than enough of Freddy for one day. "Give it a rest," Troy said wearily. "I'm stayin' right here. That wash doesn't go anywhere. It's not like the mouth of a creek or anything."

I didn't know what to do. But like everybody else, I was too tired even to think. Probably nothing was going to happen to us. It wasn't worth the effort under these conditions. We let the night come.

Adam was trying his best to be brave, but anyone could see his shoulder was terribly painful. "I could try to fix it for you," Freddy said.

"You're kidding."

"I might make it worse, but probably I can pull it back in."

"You've done this before?"

"Watched my dad do it."

"To who?"

"A guy that got thrown off a horse."

"Give it a try, Freddy."

"You're sure?"

"I have a feeling that help is not on the way."

By the gas lantern, Freddy had Adam lie on his back in the sand. Freddy took off his left shoe and lay down on his own back alongside Adam, nesting his left foot in Adam's armpit. Freddy sat up a bit, took Adam's forearm with both hands and said, "Ready?"

"Is this the part about stretching ourselves?" Adam quipped.

Freddy leaned back and pulled, smoothly and decisively.

And that was it. We heard it go back in. The bone went back into its socket, and Adam could feel it as quickly as it had happened.

"How does it feel?" we were all asking.

"A lot better—like a bad ache instead of bloody murder."

"This guy's somethin' else," Rita said. "Freddy, what can't you do? Want to come back to New York with me? We could use a guy like you."

Well after dark, Star and I were finally in our bags and about to succumb to exhaustion when we heard someone moving around, coming and going from the kitchen. I wondered if the ever-ravenous Pug was wiping out the remains of our food.

The beam of my light fell on Freddy. He had one of the gas bottles in his hand. "What're you doing?" I asked him.

"Moving this stuff out of the wash." He pointed at the sky, to clouds speeding under the moon. "Look how fast the clouds are moving."

Star and I struggled out to help him. We stumbled around like sleepwalkers, but we did manage to move the most essential gear to higher ground. I'm sure everyone could hear us, but nobody else appeared. Back in our tent again, we collapsed on top of our bags, unable to muster the strength even to get inside them. "This is one pooped pup," I murmured.

"Me too. Thank God for Freddy."

"I don't even want to think of where we'd be without him."

· 15 ·

THUNDER WAS RUMBLING, MOVING OUR way. My dad and I were in a lot of trouble and we knew it. We were way above the tree line, trying to get over a pass, as the clouds were turning black and the wind began to blow. "Can't we turn back?" I pleaded, but he answered almost desperately, "It's too late now," and kept climbing with giant strides. I struggled to keep up, but I couldn't. Lightning started snapping and the thunder shook the mountains. Suddenly the swirling clouds dropped, and my dad was disappearing into the mists. "Dad!" I called. "Wait up! Wait for me!" Then he was gone, and I was running this way and that, stumbling, lost in the fog, calling his name. I caught sight of him again, nearing a lake at the bottom of the slope. The surface of the lake was all jumping with hail. As he went striding into the water, I yelled, "What are you doing?" and he said, "It's not any wetter in the lake." I saw his face for a minute but then he suddenly disappeared as the lightning struck, and I ran up and down the shore, trying in vain to catch another glimpse of him. "Dad!" I cried, "Dad!"

As I struggled myself awake, I saw the vague form of Star's face, still asleep, and I remembered where I was. My dad can't help me here, I thought. Thunder rumbled ominously, not very far away. And then again, closer. This was real thunder, not dream thunder. Star's face was suddenly illuminated as if by a flashbulb, as lighting cracked close by, and then the thunder rattled the gorge with an overwhelming concussion, like a bomb blast. Star woke, I heard curses. Suddenly the wind hit, a cyclone of a wind, and collapsed our tent around us. Before we could even react, the rain came, a raw, primal, take-no-prisoners deluge. If you're going to venture into the bowels of the earth, it seemed to say, take this! I was wide awake now.

Where to start? What could we possibly do?

Star was flailing around, elbows flying. Water was already coursing under the tent. "Stuff your sleeping bag before it gets wet," I told her, and so that's what she did. Next thing, we reached out and grabbed our sandy slickers. We pulled them on, half inside and half outside the wreck of our tent, and found ourselves standing in the downpour amidst the flashing lightning. In the earliest light of pre-dawn, punctuated by brilliant strobes of lightning, the innumerable jagged facets of the gorge were glistening like slick knives. Immediately behind our camp, sudden waterfalls were spilling off the black rock and streams were running everywhere through camp.

I saw a form running, and recognized Freddy. He grabbed a rocket box that was being swept down the creek

DOWNRIVER

that was suddenly running through the middle of our camp. I could see odds and ends out in the river, lost and gone forever, stuff we hadn't had the energy to move the night before. Troy and Pug were standing on the far side of the wash, which was running almost hip-deep. They seemed paralyzed. Freddy yelled to them to get on this side of the creek, and fast.

Freddy sprinted up the hillside to the landing where we'd stashed the group gear. Back to the beach in a few bounds with a propane bottle in each hand, he yelled, "Get what you can, get it into the boats!"

Everybody got the message. But for a moment I paused to look. In the first light of dawn, lit brighter every few seconds with flashes of lightning, monumental red waterfalls were pouring off the cliffs and into the river. Star and I scrambled our way up toward the gear, then hurtled down the disintegrating slope with it to the boats. I saw Rita's face, I saw Adam's. Everybody was working now in an amazing display of what can be done in almost no time by people who are scared out of their minds. Troy and Pug were in the boats catching gear, and the rest of us were making as many trips as we could. What little beach there had been was washing away before our eyes. Rocks were starting to tumble down among us, some as big as basketballs.

"Let's get out of here!" Rita yelled.

Then I heard a sound I'll never forget and likely never hear again: the low grinding of boulders tumbling down the wash.

Suddenly the boats were out in the middle of the river, and nobody had untied them. I saw Troy leap for the oars and Pug reached for a paddle. "Swim!" Freddy yelled, and jumped into the river. Glancing back and seeing all hell breaking loose, I realized I had only a moment, and jumped in after him.

I had no life jacket—we'd thrown them into the boats. I was swimming for my life. I looked over and saw Adam alongside me, struggling. I was able to reach the side of the paddle raft, grab Adam, and hold on to the precious chicken line. Troy was hauling Rita into the gear boat. Freddy and Pug helped Adam and me into the paddle raft. I looked back to shore. The side-stream was huge by now, flushing at high speed out of the steep draw and occupying all of what had been camp. Even above the rain I could hear the grinding of the boulders.

Star, I realized. "Oh my God, where's Star?"

It didn't matter how many times we double-checked. She wasn't in either of the boats, she was just gone. And I had promised I wouldn't let her out of my sight.

"We've done it now," I cried.

"Anybody see her get off the shore?" Troy asked.

No one had.

Numb, we floated on in the murky light, as the awareness of our loss grew and grew. No one could speak. All was black.

Rita couldn't resist. From right there in the front of Troy's boat, she turned around to Troy and said, "Freddy told you not to camp there."

"Shut up, Rita," he said wearily.

"Yeah, well, now Star's probably dead."

He took an oar off its pin, swung it, and swatted her off the front of his boat and into the river. Pug stood with his mouth agape, and the rest of us started paddling over toward Rita.

"You wouldn't listen to Freddy," I yelled at Troy, "because you always have to be in control. It's exactly what you accused Al of—only it's true of you, not him."

He stared at me like he wanted to kill me, as we pulled Rita onto the paddle raft.

"That's what it is with the maps too," I kept on. "You want everybody looking at you, not some map. You don't care about anybody but yourself. Look what you've done!"

"Jessie, you're hysterical." Troy turned his back on the paddle raft, on all of us.

I was trying to block it from my mind, but I couldn't—the Death card, the Grim Reaper astride the white horse—I had to get past the thought of it and find Star. She's all right, I told myself. We'll find her.

The rain quit as suddenly as it had begun. Shivering, we made for a rocky shore and tied up, then mechanically began stowing things away on the boats. It had to be done. Nobody did any talking. Troy and Pug were sitting off by themselves and watching us work.

In a few minutes we were back on the river, floating somberly, shivering and brooding. Pug rode with Troy.

That's when it happened—the miracle. That's when we got let off the hook that we were sure to hang from for the rest of our lives. We heard a voice calling, then again, and there stood Star, knee-deep in water at the edge of a little beach, waving her arms. "Over here! Over here!"

We were so relieved we swarmed all over her, everyone all trying to hug her at once, except for Troy who was off to the side doing his best to look vindicated.

"Hope and inspiration, Jessie," she whispered weakly. "I kept thinking I could choose to live, and I did." I put my arms around her and walked her over to a spot where we could sit down. Rita brought over a sleeping bag to use like a blanket. Star was in a daze. Adam came over and sat by her. They had both been through it.

All of us were freezing. We broke out a stove and a propane bottle and fixed some hot coffee. We couldn't get enough of it, especially Star. "Hey, Adam," Rita hollered. "Got any jokes? Give us some shtick!"

"Actually, Rita, I'm wondering about something. . . ."

Adam reached into his soggy day pack and pulled out his blue soap dish. It was dripping water as he held it out. Adam unfastened the lid, and then carefully opened it from both sides. The scorpion was sloshing around in a quarter-inch of water, which Adam poured off. Back on dry plastic, the scorpion raised its tail and squared off. "Hardy little bugger," Adam said.

Pug was looking over his shoulder. "Is he still alive? Let me see him."

Adam snapped the lid shut and put the case back in his day pack. He was awfully subdued, and had been since the day before. I'm sure his shoulder was still plenty sore, and having to swim again this morning couldn't have helped.

After changing into whatever dry clothes we could find, we got back on the river. We were almost as quiet as we'd been before finding Star. We broke out of the gorge as the clouds began to lift, and shafts of light illuminated the full width of the Grand Canyon, falling on temples, buttes, spires, and mesas floating like islands among dissolving and regathering clouds. In places we could see all the way from the river to the forest on the north rim, its tall trees cloaked with fresh snow.

Here was the Grand Canyon I'd always pictured, only glowing with more color than I could have imagined. Two rainbows appeared, seeming to draw their hues from the multicolored formations of stone, the gold clouds, purple clouds, and the blue sky. I was at the back of the boat, close to Freddy. I said, "It couldn't be more different from this morning."

He smiled and said, "Same old friends, the wind and the rain."

Another world, I thought, Freddy really does live in another world.

We ran rapids all day, including three or four that we needed to scout. Early on, Troy and Pug blasted through one of these without scouting, and after that Troy was so far ahead we couldn't even see him. We were on our own in the paddle raft, and we knew there'd be no one to rescue us if we had any trouble. I for one didn't care that Troy had left us behind—I knew he wouldn't be much help in an emergency anyway.

I caught myself starting to catalog all his faults, small and large. That I had been so impressed with him, I realized, probably says more about me than it does about him. It was so easy to just let him think for both of us. I guess I let those blue eyes get to me. Big mistake.

We put on the miles. The river was running a rich red with the flooding, and it was running high. We were back in the sunshine and feeling warmth in our bones again for the first time since we started into the gorge with Al, which seemed like another lifetime. A helicopter appeared, remaining fairly high up. As quickly as it had come, it disappeared. "They seem to be just keeping tabs," I said. "Maybe counting heads after Crystal and the weather."

Late in the day we found Troy and Pug at the mouth of a canyon where four boats were tied up at a small camp, with no people around. The canyon was discharging clear water into the red of the Colorado. The stream was the largest we'd seen since the River of Blue, and it ran pure and fast like a Rocky Mountain trout stream. Troy was acting pretty smug about it, as if he had personally discovered the good drinking water. I refrained from making any more remarks; I could see his giant ego wobbling on matchstick legs. We were thirsty, having avoided the sand-laden river water, and here was a stream the storm hadn't muddied. We filled our water jugs.

"So what was keeping you guys?" Pug said.

"Yeah, right," Rita shot back. "Thanks for watching out for us. What if we'd flipped?"

Troy said, "Put a sock in it, Rita. They can hear you back in New York."

Rita went after him that quick, and I believe she would have done some damage if we hadn't pulled her away.

"Lemme go!" she was yelling. "Think you can knock me in the river, do you? Watch it, Troy, just watch it."

"Who do you think these boats belong to?" I asked, hoping to distract them from all the hassling.

It felt strange standing around these other boats and all this equipment that was attached to other people.

"Probably some people on a hike up the canyon," Troy said.

DOWNRIVER

Troy and Pug were anxious to put back on the river, but the rest of us, happy to be off the boats, were easing our backs and stretching our legs. Freddy and Star and I were talking about going for a little walk up the stream. Rita said she was too tired to walk, and Adam couldn't; he was limping worse than before.

"Hey, we have a long way to go," Troy said.

"We won't be gone long," I said. "No more than a half an hour."

"A short hike," Troy said sarcastically. "Seems like I've heard that one before."

Star and Freddy and I walked along the stream until we came to a shelf of rock by a crystal pool, underneath a short waterfall. We took off our sneakers and rinsed our feet in the icy water, then lay back on the warm rock and basked in the sunshine. It felt so good. It was such a reprieve to be away from Pug and Troy, to try to forget for a few minutes that we weren't okay anymore. I heard the song of the canyon wren, and tried to clear my mind of the anxiety, to focus only on the wren and the cascading stream, but I couldn't.

Star and Freddy sat up. Maybe they couldn't rest either. "Look at you," Freddy said to Star. "Look at those muscles." He playfully felt her bicep. "You've been getting stronger and stronger."

Star was getting into it. "Maybe I have," she said, as she flexed one arm, then the other. "I never thought I could do all this."

"See, Star," I said. "I was right. You are going to live to be an old lady—and probably a tough old one at that."

We all got a kick out of picturing Star as this eccentric

old lady, covered with beads and bandanas, friendship bracelets up and down her legs.

As we were laughing, we heard voices. Hikers soon appeared on their way back to their boats.

A dozen or so men and women in their thirties and forties, they stopped to chat. They were so friendly and so normal, just like people from Boulder. What I couldn't get over was, they looked so clean. And the amazing part was that they were on their twentieth day of a thirty-day trip. They'd been side-hiking every canyon they could, all the way down the river, and had already spent a night here. They told us that the hike they'd just made was the most wonderful of all. Four miles up the trail, they said, a river bursts out of the redwall limestone cliffs. "It's the largest spring in the world," a woman said. She was the one I'd been watching. A radiant person, sturdy, someone obviously at peace with herself and filled with the joy of it all.

"What's it called?" I asked.

They seemed surprised that we didn't know. "Thunder River," she said. "If you guys can possibly manage the time, it really is one of the wonders of the world. Everywhere the mists from the falls touch, it's an oasis—big cottonwood trees, vines, ferns. . . ."

Freddy was wide-eyed, taking it all in.

"We're behind schedule," I said. "But we'll tell the rest of our group about it."

"How far is it to Lava Falls?" Freddy asked them.

They figured out pretty fast that we didn't have a mile-by-mile guide. "We lost it in the river," I explained.

As we walked back to the boats together, Freddy asked them how to run Lava.

"There won't be enough water for the left run," the woman told us. "You'll have to run the right, and it'll be wild. Most boats come through totally out of control, but rightside up. Actually we've had a lot more trouble in Upset—most people do. On our last trip we flipped two out of our four boats in the big hole in Upset."

"Upset," I said faintly. "Nobody even told us about Upset."

"You'll get there tomorrow. We'll give you one of our mile-by-mile guides so it doesn't sneak up on you. It's really long, and kind of on a turn. The big hole's at the bottom. It definitely deserves a good scout."

Back at the boats we joined the rest of our group. They were just hanging out, and to my surprise Troy and Pug didn't look unhappy about waiting for us. The other group started putting on their life jackets and getting ready to go. The woman I liked so much brought over the river guide and said, "I can't resist making one more suggestion. Don't miss Havasu Creek if you can help it."

The woman quickly flipped through the guide. "We're at Mile One thirty-four here—the mouth of Tapeats Creek. Upset's at one fifty. Havasu Creek is at one fifty-seven. Hug the cliffs on the left as you're getting close to Havasu. It's so narrow at the bottom that you can slide right by it. As far as you want to hike up the creek, there's one beautiful blue-green pool after another formed by natural travertine dams, and lots of waterfalls: Beaver, Mooney, Havasu. . . . Well, Havasu Falls is a bit far. It's up near Supai, the Indian village."

"Indian village?" Suddenly Troy was all ears. "Is there a road into there?"

"No, only mules and helicopters come into the village from the rim. And hikers, of course. Anyway if you got up the creek at least to Beaver Falls, it would be well worth it."

We watched their boats round a bend and disappear. I thought Troy would be anxious to get back on the river, but he said he wanted to stay right where we were for a while. That was just fine with everybody else. Maybe he's going to calm down, I thought.

· 16 ·

DINNER THAT NIGHT WAS CERTAINLY LESS than gourmet—melted cheese over rice. As we ate, the tension seemed to lift a bit. Troy and Pug were feeling better, that was easy to see. They didn't go so far as to offer to help with the dishes, but they did say a campfire would be nice, and started gathering driftwood. Pug was excited, like a little kid. "Let's get lots of wood," I heard him telling Troy. "Let's have a real bonfire."

Adam and I were doing the dishes. I was thinking how ironic it was that he was more helpful now that he was disabled than he'd been when he was healthy. He was getting around with a sturdy walking staff of tamarisk that he'd whittled with his pocket knife. "How's the shoulder?" I asked him.

"Still hurts a lot—I can't lift my arm up very high—but nothing like it did when it was dislocated. I mean, that was painful."

179

"I bet it was." I was thinking, this is the first real conversation we've had all the way down the river. I was thinking about comparing notes with him about Troy—things obviously weren't the same between them, either—but I thought better of it. "Maybe we can take a look at your foot afterwards," I suggested.

"I cleaned it and put that antibiotic stuff on while you were up the creek."

"So how's it look?"

"Fine," he said, less than convincingly.

"You're limping worse than before. Let me take another look at it."

"Really, Jessie, I already cleaned it up."

It's getting infected, I thought. My dad's like that; he doesn't want you to know when he's sick.

"I don't want to have to amputate with that rubber sword."

He smiled. "Lost it in Crystal."

It got dark, and we were all sitting around the campfire. Pug looked like the proverbial cat that ate the canary, and after a while we found out why when he brought out a quart water bottle full of a golden liquid. "Look what that other group donated to us," he said. "Tequila."

"You're kidding," I objected. "You guys ripped them off?"

"Don't get all excited, Jessie," Troy said. "Just think of it as a gift. . . . Sort of like the river guide they gave us."

"Who cares?" Rita said. "Let's have a drink."

Pug took out his big knife, stuck it between his teeth, and mumbled, "Hey, we're River Pirates, remember?"

The bottle went around once, and then Troy remembered that we had a few limes in the bottom of the cooler. He brought them over all quartered on a dish, with a salt shaker in his hand. "Let's do it up right," he said, "like they do in Mexico."

Passing the lime sections around, he said, "I'll give you a demo." He salted the crease between his left thumb and forefinger, then reached for the tequila. Everyone else was watching him. Mr. Personality, I thought. There's nothing that makes him feel better than being the center of attention, calling all the shots. Now he's reduced to calling tequila shots.

Troy licked his fist, took a swallow or two of tequila and then quickly bit into the lime, grimacing with satisfaction.

"Just like they do in Mexico. . . ." Adam repeated, as Troy passed him the bottle. Tilting the bottle toward us as he prepared to indulge, he said, "Salud, mis amigos—salud, pesetas y amor."

I was surprised to hear Star's voice from right beside me. "I didn't know you spoke Spanish, Adam."

"Accent wasn't right," Freddy said, "—sounded a little Japanese." Everyone was certainly enjoying the break in the tension. It was great to be having a bit of fun again. Maybe there was still hope for us.

Adam bowed, and passed the bottle to Rita, who looked around and said, "You know, guys, we're somethin' else. Here we are way down the Grand Canyon. We may not have kicked its butt, but I still say, we're kickin' butt."

"Rhaat onn!" Pug bellowed. "Pass the ammunition!"

"We're doing great," Troy said expansively. "We're going all the way."

"All the way to . . . where?" Star asked, wide-eyed. She

took the bottle from Freddy and took two or three gulps before she started coughing, yet still managed to bite into the lime, only remembering afterwards about the salt and finishing up all out of order, to everyone's appreciation.

Adam was cracking up.

Out of nowhere, Pug said, "There's a deep pool just up the creek a little ways."

Nobody knew what he was getting at. "So," Rita said. "So what about it?"

"Well," Pug hesitated. "I thought maybe we . . . we could go skinny-dipping."

He looked around with a big, sheepish smile on his face. "C'mon, you guys. The moon's up and everything."

Rita and I were cracking up. "In your dreams, Pug," she told him. "In your dreams."

"Seriously," I heard Troy saying as the bottle came to me again, "it's time to be thinking about what's next."

"Lava Falls," I said. "That's what's next. It's only forty-five miles away. We're at one thirty-four, and Lava Falls is at Mile One seventy-nine. What did Al call it . . . 'the steepest navigable rapid in North America'?"

Quickly I licked up the salt, took a big swallow of tequila, and bit into the lime. Steam must have been escaping from my ears. Finally I was as warm as I could want to be, with the bonfire cooking me from the outside and the tequila from the inside.

As everybody was somberly considering those two words, "Lava Falls," Troy waved his hands and said, "That's not what I'm talking about. I mean, where next after the Grand Canyon?"

He's got to be kidding, I thought.

"Paris?" Adam suggested quizzically. "Let's all go to Paris together and speak French. Go to French restaurants, order right off the menu. Wear French clothes, drink French wine, drive French cars, smoke French cigarettes. Or maybe Greece—sail around the islands in a yacht, I'd like that."

"Eating Greek food and speaking Greek," Pug suggested.

Troy was chuckling too, with the official manner of a master of ceremonies. The bottle was making its fourth trip around. Troy said quickly, while Adam was poking the fire and Pug was finishing the bottle, "I'm talking Mexico. Now listen, everybody, we've had a few disagreements, but we're awesome. All of us—I mean everybody."

Troy, I thought, you are amazing. There you go with the eyes, even trying them on me again.

"Do you realize how close the Mexican border is? Jessie, Star . . . do you have any idea how nice it is down there in the winter? Rita, Freddy, Adam . . . do you have any idea of the rate of exchange—two thousand, three thousand pesos for one dollar! We could live like kings!"

"Living like *kings,*" Adam chanted, fairly exploding with the image.

"Here he goes," said Rita appreciatively. "This guy's too much."

"Yes, my friends," Adam whispered wistfully, "We'll be living like kings . . . living in a tile-floored hacienda by the sea, with the trade winds blowing gentle breezes through the palms. Accordions playing, soft guitars strumming, castanets clicking, iguanas patrolling the rooftops. . . . We bathe in the sea, we rest in our hammocks, we sip *piña coladas* served by sandaled servants who always wear white and have big hats. The stirrers in our drinks are hand-carved from native plastic in the image of Aztec gods. Parrots warble romantic music and the servants add the harmony parts if you ask them to. There's fruit on all sides, all the fruit you can eat—papayas, mangos, and pineapples—and endless supplies of limes and tequila. Salt, naturally, and fresh fish—red snapper, sea bass, mahi-mahi—"

"We got the picture," Troy said impatiently, ignoring the possibility that Adam was putting him on. Or was it all in my tequila-fired imagination?

Anyway I was laughing, and Troy was saying, "Seriously—you guys don't understand what that rate of exchange means. You don't go to a big international resort—you go to a remote village on the beach, you rent one of those open-air houses, and you live off the local economy."

Great, I thought. Spend the rest of my life as a fugitive from justice, with Troy, in Mexico. "It must cost *something*," I objected, trying to keep a straight face.

Troy's eyes scanned us, and he said, "Hey, I got money, okay? Money's not the problem. Does anybody have a better idea? I'm not joking—I'm going to Mexico and you're all invited."

"Livin' like kings," Pug said.

Troy was looking around for his support. "We can do it."

"I know," Adam said. "I've been down there before. People are nice too. And if you get away from where the gringos are, everything costs next to nothing, it's true. Not to mention we'd be escaping justice, as they say. . . ."

"On to Mexico," Pug sang.

Adam waved the empty bottle. *"Viva Mexico!"*

Now I was all confused. Maybe Adam would do that. . . . It would be just like him.

"Rita," Troy said excitedly, "give me that river map. I got an idea."

Troy started flipping through the pages. "That other group mentioned a hiking trail that goes out Havasu Creek through some Indian village. Remember, Al is expecting us to go all the way through the canyon and take out where everyone else does, either Diamond Creek or Lake Mead. Here it is—we'll hit Havasu Creek tomorrow."

"Look who's all into the mile-by-mile guide," Star said, and pointed at Troy. She said it loud and clear. Tipsy, but loud and clear. She was getting really spunky.

Troy looked up, astonished to realize that Star, of all people, was making fun of him.

"Hey, I know why we're working on a new plan," Rita shouted, tickled with some great insight of her own. "*Troy's afraid of Lava.* Troy's afraid to run Lava Falls after the flip in Crystal! That's why he wants to go out Havasu Creek! Didn't like that spin in the washing machine, eh, Troy?"

Troy lost it. He jumped up and stood in front of Rita, who was rapidly scrambling to her feet. "Maniac," she said, "can't you take a joke?"

Troy pushed her suddenly, and she went sprawling down into the sand, catching herself on her hands.

Rita was scrambling to her feet again, and so was everybody else, trying to back up and get out of the way.

"Party's over," Freddy said, stepping forward. "Let's call it a night."

"Who says it's over?" Troy snarled. "Nothing's over till I say it's over."

"Yeah," Pug said, swaggering into the clearing. "Who says it's over? Freddy?" He drew his knife from its sheath, and said, "From now on, you're going to do whatever Troy tells you to do. Got it, punk?"

Pug was waving the big knife back and forth for emphasis, swaying a little from the tequila. Just that quick Freddy struck, and the knife went flying. In a few seconds, as we watched with our mouths open, Pug lay wheezing on the ground. Nobody reached for the knife, certainly not Troy. He'd backed away, and there was more moonlight than firelight on his face.

Hurt and drunk, Pug was having a hard time picking himself up. Freddy picked up the knife, took a few steps, held it by the tip of the blade, and sent it flying end over end into the river. Everyone could hear the splash. Freddy said, "I'm tired of looking at that thing."

Troy grabbed Adam's walking stick away from him. He was watching Freddy and Pug both, trying to gauge how soon his Goliath was going to recover. Rita reached down for a rock, grabbed a second one and handed it to me.

Pug was back on his feet, but he didn't look much like a warrior. Troy threw the staff down and muttered, "Such a bunch of losers I never saw in my life."

Troy and Pug went down to the beach together and were carrying on quite a discussion, plotting their revenge, no doubt. Some tough guys, I thought. I'm not impressed. I thought we should get away from them a little, where we could talk among ourselves. We started to walk up the creek. "My foot's hurtin' too bad," Adam said. "I'm going back to the fire."

"I'll stay with Adam," Rita said.

DOWNRIVER

We sat on the slickrock by a little pool along the creek, just the three of us again. For a long while, we didn't speak. The nearly full moon lit up the canyon walls and the river and our faces. It was a cold moon, and I was afraid.

"Freddy," Star said finally, "you have to watch out for those guys. There's no telling what they might do."

"I'm not afraid of guys like that."

"It's Troy," she said, all serious. "He really has it in for you."

"If those two hike out Havasu Creek tomorrow," I said, "it's none too soon for me."

"Maybe we should all go out Havasu Creek," Star suggested. "Give them a head start, so we won't have to be with them, and then go up ourselves. Adam's hurt . . . we're just putting off the inevitable."

"You mean, turning ourselves in," I said.

"What else are we going to do?"

I could see that Freddy wasn't so sure about leaving the canyon just yet. But he held back, and kept his thoughts to himself.

Back in camp Star and I were just about asleep when I became aware of someone outside our tent, calling my name. It was Freddy. I struggled to my elbows and unzipped the tent. I parted the door and saw Freddy's face in the moonlight. He was in agony. "I got stung," he said. "Couple of times."

"Stung?"

"In my sleeping bag."

Poor Freddy. The thought of him being hurt had never entered my mind. I'd always thought of him as impervious to pain. He knelt on one knee, with one hand behind his back.

"What was it?" Star asked. "What stung you?"

"I don't know...," he said, his voice thick and choking in his throat. "It got me more than once—I think it must have been a scorpion."

"Oh my God," I said. "Freddy, get in here."

With our flashlights we located the stings. There were two of them, tiny bumps along Freddy's spine in the small of his back. "Star," I said, "would you get the first aid kit off the boat, and pull out the book?"

Troy did this, I thought, *I know it.*

I had Freddy crawl into Star's sleeping bag, while I scrambled out of my own. I pulled on my jeans and a sweater. Freddy's breathing was in short gasps now. "Tell me what it feels like," I asked him.

He was writhing around in the bag. I felt his forehead; he had quite a fever.

"It hurts like crazy where I was stung. . . . My throat is dry. I need a drink of water."

I handed him my water bottle, and he managed to sit up on one elbow and take a few sips. "Where's Star? What's taking her so long?" he asked.

"She'll be right here."

Parting the door, I saw Star with the flashlight in her teeth, stumbling toward us with the heavy first aid rocket box in her arms.

Back inside she was pulling on more clothes, while I was reading what the first aid book had to say about scorpion stings. It wasn't going to be much help about what to

DOWNRIVER

actually do, I could see right away. Treat for shock, it said, and get the victim to the hospital.

"What's it say?" Freddy rasped.

"It says babies are in the most trouble, because of their low body weight."

"Jessie, please read me the whole thing. I need to know."

I looked at Star, and then I read. "Of the twenty known species of scorpion in the Southwest, only one, the slender scorpion, is considered lethal. It is found mostly in southern Arizona and in the bottom of the Grand Canyon. The sting of other scorpions causes local swelling, while that of the slender scorpion is systemic, with intense pain at the site of the sting which may not abate for up to twelve hours. Small children and infants are at greatest risk due to low body weight. Multiple stings, especially around the neck or spine, can prove lethal for adults as well. Reactions vary considerably from person to person. Respiratory distress, shock, and exhaustion can lead to death. Keep the victim calm. Treat with ice at the site of the sting, treat for shock, hospitalize if possible. Several Arizona hospitals have antivenin."

"That's all?"

"That's it," I said helplessly.

"Freddy," Star said, "you're not going to die. I know it."

"Freddy grinned through his pain. "I'm not planning on it. . . . I keep thinking about something my mother told me. The Hopis get bit sometimes when they do the snake dance. I asked her why those rattlesnake bites don't make 'em sick or kill 'em. She said"—Freddy's hand emerged from the bag and pointed to his head—"the answer's up here."

"That's it," I said. "Whistle through your teeth and spit,

189

Freddy. Like your dad always used to say."

We sat beside him into the endless night. No more talking, it was too hard on him. We had no ice to put on the stings. I kept my hand on his forehead, and our eyes met often. His breathing came more and more labored as his pulse raced, and he tossed and turned with all his muscles contracting. He had retreated deep into himself, and was drawing strength from places only he knew. Sometime after the moon went down, though, it all started to back off, and eventually he was able to fall asleep. Star and I were so thankful. We kept watching him to make sure he was still breathing. I looked to Star. "He's gonna make it, Star," I whispered.

"Jessie, I think we should wake Adam and Rita. We need to tell them what's happened. I think we need to do something. We need to get away from these guys before something worse happens. I've seen people like Troy before. You have to get away from them."

The four of us gathered just outside the tent, whispering. "I already checked," Adam said first thing. "That scorpion in my blue soap dish—it's not there. They could have killed Freddy."

We were all of one mind: We had to leave as quickly as possible, and we had to take both boats so they couldn't follow us. The first light of dawn was already starting to show. We would have to be quick and very quiet. "Take your sleeping bags and clothes," I said. "There's food on the gear boat. Leave everything else behind. We can make it to Havasu Creek by this evening."

We carried Freddy, inside the sleeping bag, and slipped away onto the river.

◦ 17 ◦

"HEADIN' FOR HAVASU," I SANG SOFTLY. "We're headin' for Havasu Creek, Freddy. Home stretch."

He couldn't hear me. He was asleep, lying in the sleeping bag on top of the cooler in front of me. I was rowing the gear boat and trying to avoid any waves that would splash him. Fortunately we had no big water to run until Upset.

Upset. The name was working on me. It was down there waiting, seven miles short of Havasu. As we floated through the slow and chilly hours of the morning, I thought about what was coming. Counting me, we had only three able-bodied paddlers, and with only three paddles in the water, we wouldn't have a prayer in a major rapid like Upset. We'd all have to run it in the gear boat.

It was going to be up to me to get us through Upset. I was the only one of us who'd handled the oars. We'd deflate the paddle raft, fold it up, and leave it at Upset. Then I'd row them all through. Portaging was out. It was a twenty-three mile day to Havasu Creek. We had to get there today. It was going to be up to me.

We rounded a bend and came into the sunshine at last. Within moments I was warm. I felt good, I felt strong. I can do it, I told myself. Blue skies ahead; it won't be the kind of day we had at Crystal. I'll scout the rapid and I'll find the way and I'll bring them through to Havasu. Ten miles up the trail to the Supai village.

Freddy was stirring. Maybe it was the warmth that was bringing him around. He was trying to lift his head, and was having trouble clearing his eyes. "Easy, Freddy." I cushioned his head with my daypack. "Take your time."

A few more attempts and he was seeing me, right there, a girl with oars in her hands and the sun on her face and her heart singing like a canyon wren.

He propped himself up on an elbow.

"Welcome back, Freddy. Sure is good to see you."

"Me too," he said feebly. "I mean, it's good to see you too."

He was looking around. I could tell he was better—he wanted to look at the light on the passing canyon walls.

"Blue skies," I said. "How do you feel?"

"Like I've been beat with a stick. But the pain is gone. I never guessed there was anything like that. You wouldn't think that much pain could come out of something so little."

I handed him my water bottle and he slowly drank from it. "When you carried me—got us on the river—that was good. I remember you telling me to keep quiet."

"We don't have to worry about them anymore. We left them behind for good."

I was turning the page in the river guide.

"Where are we, Jessie?"

"From here it's only about seventeen miles to Havasu Creek. I've been thinking about Upset a lot. I can run it. We can put everybody in this boat, and I can run it."

He sat up some more, and I could see he was thinking it through for himself. "You're right," he said finally. "You can do it. I know you can, but what's this about Havasu? Hiking out? You can run Lava too . . . we could see the rest of the canyon. . . ."

"You would, wouldn't you? You'd keep right on going."

"Sure. When are we going to get another chance?"

"You're unbelievable. You'd go the rest of the way on a piece of driftwood. We could tie you down and let you float right on through Lava Falls all the way to Lake Mead."

"Sounds good to me."

"I read in the guide about a woman back in the 1940s who ran sixty miles of the river down below Lava in just her life jacket."

"Toss me overboard," Freddy said with a chuckle.

"Sorry, you're stuck with us, and we have this thing about eating. We're three-quarters starved and we had to leave the stoves and the pots and pans behind."

"Darn."

"I hate to get serious, but I'm worried about Adam's foot—about gangrene. And I'm thinking that maybe you should still get some medicine, the sooner the better."

He was sitting up straight now, and the other boat had seen him. They shouted and came paddling hard. I pulled into an eddy so they could catch up.

We held the boats together and basked in each other's company. I expected Rita would be shouting to the canyon rims, but this morning she was more like Star, quietly celebrating Freddy's return. We shared a feeling at this moment that was inseparable from the water and the light and the canyon. I thought about how, not so long ago, I'd thought of my future as a black tunnel. Now it was all light, with the promise of living in this kind of light.

How close we'd become. We were all looking to each other, realizing the same thing. I was taking each of them in and savoring the moment. Adam, so full of life. Freddy, born for the wild places. Rita, the irrepressible. Star, my sister.

It was Adam who put the feeling into words, as the five of us floated down the river with one heart· "I love you guys."

"Me too," Rita said. "I want to take you all back to New York."

"Hold the garlic," Adam said. "Definitely hold the garlic."

I looked across to Star, and our eyes met. She was looking a little lost, and I have an idea she was thinking how it was all coming to an end real soon.

"Hey, you guys," Rita said. "We just figured out it's November already. Can you believe that?"

Using the guide, we counted off every side-canyon marking our approach to Upset. When we first heard the River Thunder, and started into the pooled-up water behind the rapid, my heart raced. Then I felt a calm lifting me up, and I knew I wouldn't go brain dead when the test came, the way I did on Storm King. I'd come too far. I had a vision of a piece of safe water, to the side of that big hole in Upset, and I was going to reach it.

I never found out if I could have. There'll be other tests as important for me, maybe not as physical, but I'll recognize them when I see them and apply my Upset strategy.

"Helicopter," Star said, pointing.

Yes, there it was, a metal dragonfly on a ledge on river right. At the landing for the scout, two men stood waiting.

We pulled our boats together and let them drift silently with the slow current, and we cried our tears.

"It's been nice," Rita said finally. "I'm never going to forget it, that's for sure."

One of the two men was Al. The pilot wore a Park Service uniform.

The boats bumped the shore side by side, our last landing. Al and the park ranger stood back as Star and Rita tied up the boats. Adam hopped ashore and I stuck close to Freddy as he tried out his legs.

The park ranger's face registered only disapproval. I met Al's eyes as I walked up to him. The hurt was still there, but he was happy to see us, even after everything. "Freddy and Adam should go first," I said. "They should get to a hospital. Freddy got stung last night by that slender scorpion."

"Troy and Pug did it," Rita said. "Put it in Freddy's sleeping bag. They coulda killed him, and they better pay for it. They're old enough to be tried as adults, aren't they? Tell him how it all happened, Jessie."

I filled in the details, and Al listened carefully. When I was done, he said, "I hope there's a way to prove it, I really do. What do you think, Freddy?"

He shrugged. "Pretty hard to prove it was the same scorpion."

"They're up at Tapeats Creek," Rita told the pilot.

"We know," he said. "The other helicopter is picking them up. Let's get these two to the hospital."

Quickly I asked, "Are we going to see them again? Be with them somewhere?"

"Not unless you're going to the hospital in Flagstaff. Hurry up and get their personal stuff, and let's go."

My mind was numb as I packed Freddy's things into one dry bag. He sat on the shore with his head down. There was so much I wanted to say to him, so much that had been unsaid ever since the first. I carried his dry bag up the beach, handed it to the pilot, and then helped Freddy up. Adam was limping toward the helicopter. He turned and looked back at the rest of us, and stopped. For once he had nothing to say.

Freddy was on shaky legs. "Do you need some help?" I asked him.

I found his soft dark eyes. "I got it," he said. "Thanks, Jessie." He squeezed my hand, and he gave me a little hug. "Bye Star, Bye Rita."

The time for words was over. None of us could speak. We watched them as they hobbled to the helicopter. Adam was getting in, and Freddy was still on his way when I ran to him and said, "Freddy, I didn't say good-bye." I kissed him on the cheek, and he smiled.

"One more thing," I said. "Don't look down."

Freddy was so bashful. He smiled, and said, "You coulda rowed Upset."

We both looked over to the rapid. I could see the safe

water beside the big hole from where we were standing. "You coulda rowed it no problem."

We stood back with Al and watched them take off.

"Down to three," Star sighed. "How long can we stay together?"

"Tonight you'll be at a juvenile detention center in King-man. After that there's no telling. A judge will have to decide that."

Al seemed so sad. I felt as sorry for him as for me. I hugged him, and then I said, "I've learned more down here than I could ever tell you. Thanks."

He shook his head and scratched his gray, three-day beard. "I can see that's true. But don't you go telling any-body that the program still works when I'm not along, okay? I wouldn't want that to get around."

We went to work deflating the boats, rolling them up, and repacking our dry bags. It was good to have something to do. Then the other helicopter arrived, and the pilot said he'd taken Pug to Park Service Headquarters on the rim. But they hadn't been able to get Troy; he'd run off up the Thunder River Trail.

"Sounds like Troy," Al said. "They'll be waiting for him at the rim."

We climbed into the helicopter, and as we lifted up we waved to Al standing below with all his gear. The layers of the canyon opened and spread out as we climbed. I was remembering it all, from the moment we sneaked onto the river, but mostly I remembered a night under the stars, when Star had given me her friendship bracelet, and I remembered rock-hopping with Freddy up the River of

Blue. Somehow, I promised myself, I won't lose them.

"Take a look at Lava Falls," the pilot said. "There it is, that white band across the river."

"Holy cow," Rita protested. "That doesn't look like anything. I still say we coulda kicked its butt."

· 18 ·

IT WAS MARCH, LATE IN THE MORNING after a heavy spring snow, and the sun was blazing. All around us, the pines were shedding their snow and their branches were lifting, suddenly free of the weight they'd been carrying. The canyon stream was running high and brown with snowmelt. Star and Madeline and I had been out on our cross-country skis, enjoying the sunshine, and now we were headed home. We paused as the house came into sight, "the Hacienda" as we all called it, and took it in. There it was, sitting on a little hill among the pines on the sunny side of the canyon, perched above the stream. Our new home. To me the newness was part of what I loved about it. I would always have that feeling of starting fresh here.

I looked to Star and Madeline. We were all smiling, reflecting each other in our sunglasses. I had an idea they were feeling the same way about the Hacienda. How un-

199

likely that we'd come together, how well it had been working, how new it still was for all of us.

We skied down the canyon and up to the house. "I'm starved," Madeline said, stepping out of her skis. "How about you?"

"Let's fix those sandwiches," Star said, heading for the kitchen.

I poured a couple of soft drinks and brought one out for Dad in the sunroom, where he was reading the papers. My bare feet felt so good on the warm Mexican tiles. "It was wonderful out there, Dad. So warm."

"The snow's going to go fast."

I sat close to him, in one of the leather chairs. "Here's the first installment on lunch. Madeline and Star are fixing some sandwiches."

"Thanks. I've really been enjoying myself just being lazy this morning."

"I really do love this place, Dad. Especially all the light. I was thinking when I was out skiing, I had no idea it would turn out like this when it was in the planning stages."

He could see I was talking about *back then*.

Cautiously he said, "I didn't know it would turn out this well either."

"But you hoped it would. I didn't think there was anything good about it. I didn't even want to look at it."

"I remember that vaguely. . . ."

"You remember that well, Dad. I was a hard case."

"That was back when you were fifteen. Pre–Grand Canyon. What I really like about sixteen is how we can talk—you know, every so often, like now. It's great."

"I just wish I didn't have to wait another whole year to

get my driver's license. It'd be so much easier if I could drive."

"We don't mind driving you, really. This year'll fly by before you know it. You won't have this probation hanging over your head; you'll be a free woman. It's going to come too fast for me, Jessie. I want to hang on to you, both of you."

"It was great you got to meet Freddy too, after all the stories we've told about him."

"I'm glad we took that trip. He's just as you described him, maybe even better. What a break for Freddy that they sent him to southwestern Colorado to get 'rehabilitated.' He sure loves those mountains. You can see it in his eyes when he talks about the country they've been in, learning to fight the fires."

"I guess it's really hard work they do," I said, "but Freddy doesn't mind that. And if he does really well, he'll get to try out for the Forest Service Hot Shots. It's a special team of firefighters that travels all around the West fighting the worst forest fires, jumping out of planes and all that."

"Well, I hope he makes it."

"Oh, he will. And he wants to come up here some time too, and visit us. We'd like to plan a hike together, off the north rim of the Grand Canyon and down to Thunder River. He's determined to see that place one way or another. Maybe we could all go. What do you think?"

"Sounds great—that's where the underground river comes shooting out of the cliffs, isn't it? And that's the trail where Troy disappeared."

Star and Madeline brought in the sandwiches on a big tray with melon cubes around the outside and chips and guacamole in the center. Dad's eyes lit up. Chips and guacamole are his "natural food."

Star heard the sound of a vehicle stopping at the driveway. "The mail," Star said. "I'll get it."

With a spring in her step, she was out of the house. I've never seen anyone get so excited about getting mail, even junk mail. In a minute she was back, waving a letter in her hand. "Jessie! It's a letter from Adam!"

"Well, read it!"

"Okay, okay," Star said, catching her breath. "Here goes. . . .

Dear Star and Jessie,

What a flash it was to hear from you—and thanks for sending the pictures of your place. I practically karate-chopped a tree into splinters when I read that you two wound up together. I always thought you seemed like sisters anyway.

No, I haven't heard from Rita either, except that she's back in New York. And thanks for all the news about Freddy. I miss you guys, and I wish I could join you for that Thunder River hike, but not this time.

Yes, I'd wondered too if we'd ever hear what became of Troy. When I heard they didn't catch him, I could almost see him, down there in Mexico, "living like a king."

Well, ladies and gentlemen, wonder no more. Troy has been found. No, he's not passing the time in his beach hammock, sipping piña colonics and sending his servants out for red snapper. He's been in L.A. all this time. No imagination, eh? They caught him last week in Malibu, by following the trail of his credit card receipts, wouldn't you know. His parents are coming back from Europe for the occasion. Al's convinced them it's time to put Troy's feet to the fire.

How do I know all this stuff? I just heard it last night. Believe it or not, my folks and I have been in touch with Al. Yes, the very same. Now get this: I'm going to be working for Al this summer at Hoods in the Woods, as a kitchen slave and all-around go-fer! He runs a much bigger program in the summer than when we were there. Imagine, I'm going to be back in Colorado, and getting paid for mountain climbing and rafting, besides the scullery work. Kind of a junior counselor too, the idea being that if this fool can get something out of the program, anybody can.

Yes, I said rafting! We are, believe it or not, going to attempt the Mighty Canyons of the San Juan, not once but three times during the summer. Al swears by that river, so I'm looking forward to seeing it. And we'll be doing Westwater too.

I hope I'm making both of you sick and that you'll come to visit me at Discovery Unlimited. (I better start using the real name—I'm one of the staff!)

Here's my hidden agenda: One day I'm going to be a big-time river guide on—you guessed it—the Grand.

Love to you both, and here's to this crazy dream of mine, that one day the five of us will once more run the Grand Canyon of the Colorado.

Love,

Adam

P.S. This time, we'll launch in broad daylight.

"That was quite a letter," Madeline said. "You two sure wound up with some great friends."

"Friends and family," Star said, with her green eyes shining. She pulled something out of her jeans pocket and held it up for us to admire. It was another of those friendship bracelets she'd been weaving. I still had the one on my wrist that she'd given me in the Canyon.

"Whatcha got there, Star?" Dad asked.

Star sat down, then tied the new bracelet around her ankle. Silver, speckled with blue. "There," she said, hitching up her jeans a bit to reveal her now-completed collection. "Four of them—each with our soul colors. One for every member of our family."